T0110969

THE TRAGEDY OF THE STUPID NATION

Max-Landry KASSAÏ

Langaa Research & Publishing CIG
Mankon, Bamenda

Publisher:

Langaa RPCIG
Langaa Research & Publishing Common Initiative Group
P.O. Box 902 Mankon
Bamenda
North West Region
Cameroon
Langaagrp@gmail.com
www.langaa-rpcig.net

Distributed in and outside N. America by African Books
Collective
orders@africanbookscollective.com
www.africanbookscollective.com

ISBN-10: 9956-551-74-0

ISBN-13: 978-9956-551-74-3

Content

This book is dedicated to the victims of the crises in the Central African Republic

Acknowledgments

My sincere thanks go to Catherina Wilson, without whom this book would not have been possible. She gave me a taste for writing and helped me to complete this first book. Many thanks also to Professor Mirjam de Bruijn and Dr Jonna Both for their close collaboration and extensive support. Also, I cannot forget Didier Kassaï for his advice and his excellent cover design, as well as Pacôme Pabandji for his participation in the production of this book. Finally, a big kiss to my beloved daughter, Divine Alice, who gives me the smile and the strength to continue.

Max-Landry Kassaï

Note from the editor
Catherina Wilson

Max and I first met in Kinshasa in May 2014. At the time, he had already been living in the Congolese capital as a refugee for some months, and I was at the beginning of my PhD trajectory, wishing to research Central African Republic (CAR) refugees. I thought I needed to travel to the border area between CAR and Congo to meet these refugees, and thus a passage through Kinshasa for administrative and logistical purposes seemed obligatory. I had been in Kinshasa on several occasions in the past and knew people that could help me. Such was the case of Aristote Gardinois Makola, one of my Kinois 'brothers'. Having just finished a degree in communication— meaning he had time to spare—he accompanied me around town. Aristote turned out to be more than an assistant; he was a key informant and, as I would learn (in hindsight, as we always do), a gatekeeper to interesting people—and on more than one occasion.

Aristote had overheard Patricia, one of his neighbours, mentioning that Radio Elikya (the Catholic radio station where she worked) had a CAR refugee in their midst. As I told Aristote about my research plans, he immediately made the connection and put me in contact with Patricia. And so the ball started rolling. Patricia then took me to the radio premises, where Max and I met. I remember seeing him standing in the corridor: a slim young man wearing an orange t-shirt, gentle and well-spoken. In a city of over ten million inhabitants, our paths crossed—as it often happens in anthropological research—serendipitously. There are not many CAR refugees in Kinshasa, a couple of hundred at most. Meeting Max felt like finding the golden needle in the haystack, and thus I decided to postpone my trip to northern Congo.

Having worked as a journalist in Bangui, Max arrived at Radio Elikya looking for a job, where he ended up working voluntarily. His Congolese colleagues gave him the name 'Michel Djotodia'— quite unsuitable, to be honest. Max had in fact fled the Seleka rebellion led by Djotodia in May 2013. He seemed to fervently miss his life back home. Yes, he had fled war and violence in the first place, but this book shows us that this was not the only reason for flight. Max was fleeing year upon year of violent experiences and memories of them, experiences coloured by a lack of opportunities and by deep frustration. In the many conversations we had, I understood Max was fleeing in order to follow his heart. In fact, flight can never be explained by a single cause. Why do some people decide to leave, while others decide to stay? I believe that gaining insight into the layered context of the country—into the depths of individual life stories, the past, the memories, the fears, the emotions, the future perspectives, the contradictions—may help us to understand not only flight and refuge, but also migration, a topic that has become so pertinent in recent years. Stories, both imagined and real, such as the ones related in this book, invite us to have a look into this layered reality.

Working from dawn to dusk at Radio Elikya (*elikya* means 'hope' in Lingala) at times without remuneration,[1] Max felt exploited and grew even more disillusioned with Kinshasa. The refugee procedures he tried to initiate, in the hope of resettlement, were not bearing any fruits either. In fact, the UNHCR[2] policy in DR Congo amounted to helping refugees in refugee camps only—and not outside the camps, nor in terms of higher education.[3] Urban refugees, such as Max, had to learn to fend for themselves. In this book, we read that Max passed through the Mole refugee camp, where he lived for a couple of months. He describes the lack of infrastructure, the poor medical treatment, and also the boredom and the hopelessness he experienced while being there. Going back to the camp to sit around idling was not an option. '*L'exile n'est pas facile,*' I often heard CAR refugees say, echoing the words of the late CAR president, Ange-Félix Patassé, during his exile. Feeling defeated, Max decided to go back to Bangui, a city that after the Seleka coup had gone through another wave of violence: the brutal reprisals of the anti-Balaka. The country Max was about to go

---

[1] Working voluntarily at the radio station gave Max an occupation but not a means of living. Patricia earned an average Congolese salary, somewhere between 50 USD to 100 USD per month, on which it is impossible to survive in Kinshasa.
[2] The UN refugee agency: United Nations High Commission for Refugees.
[3] Refugee camps offer primary and sometimes secondary schooling.

back to was deemed by UN experts to be heading toward a genocide. Nevertheless, Max decided to return voluntarily to his country. He was one of the first refugees I knew to return, but he was certainly not to be the only one. The lack of opportunities in Kinshasa forced many others to follow in his footsteps.

While the trip from Bangui to Kinshasa had taken him months—with long stays in the refugee camp, travelling on muddy roads or in risky, over-loaded boats, and dealing with greedy police officers—Max returned to Bangui in a single day. He left Kinshasa in August 2014. At dawn, he first boarded a humanitarian flight which took him to Libenge. He then drove in a humanitarian 4x4 truck from Libenge to the Mole refugee camp, where he jumped on the back of a motorcycle taxi to Zongo, the Congolese town opposite Bangui. Here he finally took a pirogue to cross the Ubangi River and set foot in Bangui at dusk. When using the infrastructure set up by the humanitarian agencies, Bangui does not seem that far from Kinshasa. The means of transport available to the majority of people, however, stand in stark contrast to the travel realities of humanitarian agents.

While in Kinshasa, many refugees were apprehensive, and understandably so, of me. Max was in fact one of the first ones to trust me—perhaps because we had met outside the humanitarian agency context, perhaps because he needed a listening ear. Our topics of conversation, which we often held during long walks in the city, touched upon politics, the delicious food in Bangui, and also upon making decisions. Max would often ask my opinion and advice about many things. I felt respected, like an older sister, and slowly but surely our friendship grew. Back in Bangui, Max and I kept in sporadic contact (through phone and especially through social media). In 2016 I became part of the two-year research project 'Being Young in Times of Duress',[4] which focused on youth in CAR. The project was aimed at understanding what it means to be young in CAR in times of hardship and duress. Thanks to this project, we were able to work out a way to support Max in his writing of this book. While the research project increasingly focused on demobilized youngsters, Max's book provides the narrative of a boy growing up into a young man caught in extremely difficult circumstances. The latter experience has, unfortunately, been in one way or another the lot of so many youngsters in CAR.

In 2016 (and later in 2018) Max and I met in Bangui, Max's hometown, the city we had so often talked about in Kinshasa. Our meeting was full of reminiscences, melancholic, and pervaded by a feeling of being forlorn. I saw Bangui through his eyes, a less perfect Bangui than the one he had drawn

---

[4] 'Being Young in Times of Duress' was a two-year project (2016–2018) financed by the Nationale Postcode Loterij (NPL) through UNICEF Netherlands and carried out by researchers from the African Studies Centre based in Leiden, The Netherlands, in close collaboration with researchers and students from the Department of Anthropology at the University of Bangui.

for me in Kinshasa. Bangui had changed, and Max had changed too; but the lack of opportunities seemed to remain a constant given. After his return, Max had taught at a school, had worked in local NGOs, had returned to the journal he previously worked for, and had set up with friends an organic garden on his grandmother's land, on which he worked with dedication. But Max again grew frustrated; he felt stuck. Neither Bangui nor Kinshasa offered him the opportunities he was looking for.

This time he did not cross the river but found refuge in blogging, and it is his blogging that laid the basis for this book. Writing was something he had wanted to do for a long time; it was a passion. As a young boy studying in the seminary with the priests, he had learned to keep a diary. He kept little pieces of text with him, which he had lost during his flight in 2013. In Kinshasa, Max had shown me some of his texts and poems. I encouraged him to start a blog. Almost two years later, in early 2016, after a couple of aborted blogging attempts, but also in the context of upcoming and much-discussed democratic elections, Max took blogging[5] more seriously and was not afraid to express his opinion.

The project 'Being Young in Times of Duress' allowed us to finance Max's blog. We bought a computer and paid for the editing and translation of this book. In addition, the project gave us the opportunity to travel to Bangui. But above and

---

[5]Le Chroniqueur Centrafricain:
http://lechroniqeurcentrafricain.over-blog.com/

beyond these material benefits, the most enriching result, for both sides, was the collaboration (and perhaps even co-creation) that grew out of it: the ideas that were exchanged, the moral support, the advice, the lessons learned. My role in relation to Max continuously changed: I started off as a researcher, but then became a facilitator, connecting people, and even a first-hand editor. Max, at first an informant, turned into a blogger, a guide, and a writer. We became friends.

Even if Max is, without doubt, the sole author of the book, you (the reader) are holding in your hands the physical result of a co-creative endeavour. This collaboration is not limited to the exchanges between Max and me, but extends well beyond that. It is not a book written by one hand, but the result of a multi-disciplinary effort—partly artistic, partly journalistic, and partly academic. The collaboration includes, directly and indirectly, the project's research team members (in particular Jonna Both and Mirjam de Bruijn),[6] as well as the CAR cartoonist Didier Kassaï (who drew the wonderful front cover) and the CAR journalist Pacôme Pabandji (who wrote the foreword)—and not to forget the two language editors and translators, Ruadhan Hayes and Moussa Fofana, for whom translating a work of popular art was a challenge. The roles of Aristote Gardinois

---

[6] Other team members include: Marius Crépin Mouguia, Marie-Louise Esther Tchissikombre, Wilfried Vianney Poukoulé, and Jean Bruno Ngouflo–all at the Department of Anthropology at the University of Bangui; and the independent ethnographic filmmaker, Sjoerd Sijsma.

Makola and Patricia must also be recognized, as well as Max's comrade-in-arms Ephraim Tote, with whom he fled Bangui and travelled to Kinshasa. My sincere acknowledgments go to each and every one of them.

Last but not least, a note on this book's genre. The work of Max is challenging to read. For one, its style is eclectic—an amalgamation of prose, fiction, political analysis and opinion, report style with recommendations, blogging, poetry, and more. It is partly autobiographical, yet at the same time it combines a range of voices. Not everything written here has been experienced by Max in person, though elements from his own life are woven into the text. The tone of the book is gloomy, and there are many passages describing violence in a level of detail that some readers would rather omit. In all honesty, I struggled with the recurrence of these passages; however, removing them would not do justice to Max's voice and the effect on him of what happened in his country, and thus we decided not to interfere too much in what can be considered an artistic production. One can ask oneself if there are better ways to write about fear, loss, anger, crude violence … than the one here presented. Perhaps this book is best read as a product of popular culture, a genre which develops perspectives on topics that people themselves feel are interesting, attractive, or important (Barber 2018: 3)[7]—a genre that stands close to the people it describes, that depicts reality as

---

[7] Karin Barber (2018) *A History of African Popular Culture*, Cambridge University Press.

it is lived, with all its shortcomings, all its joys and sorrows.

Foreword

Pacôme Pabandji

On this evening in May, the sky gradually darkens over Bangui. Everything seems peaceful and silent. Between the banks of the Ouango River and the heat of the high flames of the *chouateries* of Lakwanga, there are even sinister locations that give one cause for fear. And yet, in front of the Mbiyé dance-bar in the Lakwanga district, the atmosphere is at its peak. A play of light, music, movements ... a complete cocktail for a perfect evening. I have arranged a meeting this evening with Catherina Wilson, who arrived in Bangui a few days earlier. We are to have a drink and talk. But when I arrive: surprise! I meet a whole team of friends, even virtual ones from social networks. When I get off the motorcycle taxi that brought me there, a thin but elegant man greets me. He introduces himself: 'My name is Max-Landry Kassaï.' His name reminds me of the famous Central African cartoonist, Didier Kassaï, with whom I have rubbed shoulders. 'No, I'm not him! It's just a homonym.' We all laugh.

This is the first time I have met this young Central African prodigy, on an evening when in some parts of Bangui the laughter is replaced by the sounds of Kalashnikov gunfire. And yet, we are already acquainted with each for a long time, thanks to the magic of social networks. But tonight's meeting is a little special. Our cool beers do not prevent us from knowing that things are going badly in Bangui; the country is in trouble. A few days earlier, the whole city of Bangui had been plunged into renewed violence. A Muslim militia had attacked the Catholic Church of Fatima when the faithful were at worship. Many people died; many others lost limbs. People fled again, to escape the law of machetes. Bangui and the whole country have been living under this law for five years now.

What Bangui is experiencing this month is only part of what Max-Landry has been going through since 2013, the year in which a Muslim-majority rebellion seized power in the Central African Republic, overthrowing François Bozizé. And yet, on this evening, he is all smiles—as if he wishes to forget all those years of horror. As if the cries of distress of his relatives and friends killed under the slashing machetes no longer echo. At his table, I meet acquaintances: Central African bloggers and a taxi-man whom I met precisely in 2013 at the height of the crisis. We recall our individual moments. Everyone relates how they experienced the first moments of this stupid war. This moment allows me to understand that I am not the only one suffering from the Central African crisis on a professional and even personal level. Max-Landry's story freezes me and plunges me back into that dark moment in time when religion was the only reason to kill one's neighbour, one's childhood friend, one's rival ...

Introduction

For several decades, our country has been affected by military–political crises, which have deeply disrupted community life. Indeed, five decades have passed in a pitiful organizational vacuum, sweeping away the gains of unity, social cohesion, and secularism.

We have grown up in war, and this has shaped us in one way or another: hatred, cruelty, and violence in all its forms have suppressed what is sociable and peaceful in us. The world calls us monsters, inhuman, because we have plumbed the depths of cruelty. How can a man eat his neighbour's flesh? How can we enter into a village to massacre all those who do not share our beliefs?

So many other questions could be asked to illustrate the most serious of all the crises our country has experienced. But we must immediately understand that these respective crises stem from the poor organization and opaque management of our country. No man can claim to lead a people if he does not have the sense to gather, to unite around him all the different social strata. During these five decades, we have witnessed a chaos of political structuring, committed to nepotism, clanism, and regionalism— all of which has led to the abandonment of certain ethnic groups and minorities.

In this way, the provinces and villages are completely neglected by the central government, whose management is characterized by corruption, the misappropriation of public funds, and the poor distribution of the country's wealth. There is no equality of opportunity or treatment before the public services of the state. As a result, the method of recruitment within these services or in the general administration is not based on criteria of competence or merit. On the contrary, access to positions of responsibility generally involves nepotism.

As a result, and at a certain point, people's exasperation becomes widespread and rebellions in the cities follow one another—because a significant number of unemployed young people are beginning to join rebel movements to enable a radical change. In the end, the interests of some cannot be reconciled with those of others who are demanding power or a broad representation of their community. As a result, community tensions arise due to the marginalization of those who are under-represented.

And so we have experienced the most horrific crisis in our history: the Seleka–Antibalaka war, which has led to the breakup of our society.

This narrative deals with the political and social problems of the Central African people. As such, it seeks to denounce the abuses of power, the failures in the management of public resources, and the marginalization of certain under-represented communities. It therefore aims to contribute to the improvement of people's living conditions, respect for public freedoms and fundamental human rights, equal distribution of the country's wealth, and the integration of all in the national development process.

This narrative is an undertaking that wishes to help restore peace, social cohesion, and the full integration of all communities through our commitment to raising people's awareness of the problems that afflict them.

We cannot accept that our state is poorly governed and that people are marginalized. We have had narrow, greedy state thieves who have wallowed in luxury at the expense of the people. And here, we report the damaging effects of the injustice, impunity, and appalling inequalities that have led us into horror.

Chapter 1

The sky was a little threatening, and large masses of cloud covered part of the blue overhead. Bangui became subdued as a result. It was 1:30 p.m. An unusual silence seemed to be spreading in our neighbourhood. I came out of my room after a difficult nap. I felt that everything was moving, that everything was in motion. People were running all over the place and cars were flying by at full speed. I asked why the neighbourhood was so quiet?

Near me there was a group of young people playing checkers. One of them answered me: 'Don't you know that we are in a country of madmen? There are no dumber people than we Central Africans. A new coup d'état has just been botched.' He uttered an innocent little cry and his face was covered with sadness.

A few minutes later, we saw a group of loyalist soldiers sweeping through the streets. They were all on duty. People on all sides were looking to return home as quickly as possible. A rhythm of control was imposed. All passing vehicles had to undergo a strict inspection. At 3 p.m. the president, against whom the coup d'état had just failed, issued a statement: 'Dear compatriots, Central African people. We have just foiled a coup d'état that was carefully prepared by a group of people from the Yaki ethnic group. And they have long wanted to overthrow me, after their defeat in the last presidential election. So I know them all, and I promise you that they will have to answer for their actions before the courts. I will be ruthless toward them, and I will deploy all the means I have in my possession to hunt them down.'

Immediately, the whole city was in turmoil. The soldiers increased their patrols in the neighbourhoods, while searching the cars and bags of passers-by. We lived in the city's 7th *arrondissement*, where the residence of the deposed president was and where there were a significant number of people of the Yaki ethnic group.

Our *arrondissement* was surrounded. No one could enter or leave because of the directive issued by the president. The soldiers began to enter into the neighbourhoods to extract half-naked people. This commotion became terrible, and gunfire of all calibres began to be heard. The arrested persons were formed into a line and marched in single file to climb into large loyalist military vehicles prepared for the occasion. They were loaded into these vehicles and driven off to an unknown destination. Already, on the spot, the loyalist soldiers began to beat them with their rifle butts, tying them up savagely. As a result, some of them were injured and lost a lot of blood.

We could hear from afar what these loyalist guards were saying: 'We must take these men away. They're the ones who want to undermine our system. We'll eliminate all of them, those who believe they're the most intelligent ethnic group and superior to ours.'

A crowd of women were shouting their heads off: 'Let all the men leave their homes and save themselves, because the military is conducting a manhunt!'

The soldiers went door-to-door in their hunting. The neighbourhoods were emptied of their inhabitants. Most of the men in this *arrondissement* had to flee far away, into the mountains and the forests to hide, to protect themselves from being murdered, abandoning their women and children.

Night had fallen, and the profound silence of a cemetery settled over the almost deserted neighbourhoods. There were some women to be seen, those who went out to look for oil from the sellers because the electricity was cut off and it was very dark outside. Only a few stars shone in the sky. That night, a blaze of violence erupted. The men who could not escape were subjected to barbarity, to the cruelty of these armed men. It was a hideous massacre, when some of these armed men—gathered into a small brigade supposedly to repress banditry—set about torturing those who could not escape, subjecting them to all kinds of degrading treatment.

Our house contained a reinforced basement, whose main door was in our bathroom. It was very difficult to detect; and we, the children of this family, learned of it only on that day. Papa had never told us about such a place before. It was kept secret. It was a corner more than six metres deep, consisting of three rooms serving as bedrooms and a living room. It was almost empty, containing only one dusty piece of furniture.

Mama took charge of lowering our mattresses down into the basement and spreading them out on the floor. I was barely 12 years old and my sister was two years younger. We surrounded our parents that day, and we began to pester them with questions about what had just happened in the country. Why this sudden change in events? Mama and Papa made no effort to mince their words. They told us things as they had happened: the reason for this failed coup d'état.

The plan was to overthrow Kota, the current president, to return power to the benefit of the Yaki ethnic group. I had never shared the view our parents wanted us to believe: that our ethnic group was superior to others.

The Yaki ethnic group are local residents accustomed to fishing and trade. They are primarily from the DRC and have a slightly light complexion. They are hard-working men who have wealth due to their fishing and trading activities. Narrow ideas of division were ingrained in us. Our hearts, minds, and souls were prepared to hate others, to despise them.

However, from a young age I understood that we were in no way superior to others—the Banda, the Gbaya, and the Kaba in particular, who came from the north. And my realization could be confirmed in reality, as I had studied and grown up with friends from these ethnic groups, who were just as bright as I was. I was led to the conclusion that this established superiority was fomented by the spirit of domination. It was the work of ancestors of our clan, who passed it on from generation to generation. And my parents had been cradled in this mistaken culture.

My father did not understand why I was reluctant to think we were superior to others. Certainly, I was strongly resistant to this falsehood. In addition, I loved all my friends, especially those in my class and in my surroundings. We had interesting recreational games in common and we shared our home-prepared lunch packs together, not to mention our hide-and-seek games. Everything was rosy; life was really beautiful.

It was very dark in the basement. Papa decided to get oil from upstairs, but he did not find any. He came downstairs to ask Mama if he could go out and buy some outside at the dealers, but her refusal was categorical. She did not want him to risk his life—because the soldiers were seizing everyone from the Yaki ethnic group. And in the face of this refusal, Papa could find nothing better to do than to do as he pleased. He decided to leave at his own risk and peril. He knew all the little corners of the neighbourhood like the back of his hand. He wormed his way through the middle of the houses which adjoined each other, to reach the commercial centre where Uncle Zada was.

As Papa went along, he heard in the half-light a small scream from under a tree. A man was getting his throat cut by the loyalists. Papa was distraught. He immediately sought to return to the basement. His whole body was drenched in sweat. He observed another group of soldiers raping a woman and a young girl. But Papa had become the epitome of helplessness, and there was absolutely nothing he could do to assist these unfortunate people, so he hurried to return home.

When he got back to the basement, he was shaking so violently that neither Mama nor anyone else could ask him any questions. We understood correctly that something must have happened to him. My little sister and I started shedding hot tears. He grabbed us by the arms and held us close to him.

After he regained his composure, he began to tell us what he had been through outside. Mama had us serve the rest of the meal we had eaten at noon; however, Papa was unable to swallow anything. The scenes he had witnessed continued to turn in his head. In the end, Mom urged us to go to bed. We willingly acquiesced. Our parents both stayed in the living room.

From a distance, one could listen quietly to a few words that escaped their conversation. Papa wished us to leave the district we were in, for another where we would be safe. He was afraid that we would not have enough food to feed ourselves. He also did not know how long this crisis could last. Mama expressed her concern about the arbitrary arrests and their unfortunate consequences. Papa simply replied that there was no choice and that we had to try to leave the *arrondissement* the following morning.

When dawn finally arose, life was slowly returning to normal. Papa went out immediately and checked on the atmosphere outside. He heard howling and weeping coming from Uncle Sam's, whose house was a few metres from ours. He understood that Uncle Sam had just been killed, which is why his house was in mourning. The atmosphere outside was very strange. Only women and children could move around—and loyalist soldiers.

Daddy retraced his steps to tell us of Uncle Sam's death. At this news, Mama fainted, because Uncle Sam was her older brother by three years. Papa tried to revive her. As for us, we started to cry. We were also very close to our uncle. Papa managed to bring Mama around, but she could not immediately recover all her senses—because she and Uncle Sam had been so close. Nevertheless, she managed to console us, as we had thrown ourselves on the ground in tears.

When Mama had recovered somewhat, Papa insisted that she pack our bags in order to leave for the 4th *arrondissement*. However, he could not go with us because of the risks associated with arbitrary arrest, so it was a very painful separation and affected us a lot. But we understood the necessity of this decision, and no one could question it. Our belongings were packed and we had to get up early in the morning to leave. We kissed him and he clasped us to him. A short prayer was said, and he let us go up the basement steps.

Chapter 2

What a commotion! A huge crowd of displaced people, all from our *arrondissement*, were swarming along the Ndress road that led to the 4th *arrondissement*. We therefore understood that we were not the only ones leaving to seek shelter from violence. Among us were women, children, and a few old people. Adult men could not pass that way because they would simply be arrested. Friends formed into groups along the route. In this way, we reunited with some of the families with whom our parents had been acquainted.

All those who had set out had something in common: they were grief-stricken, people who bore heavy sorrows for those who had been close to them and had been murdered. They had not finished mourning over them or burying them with dignity, but were forced to set off in order to protect themselves from violence and massacre.

A woman among the crowd kept crying. She seemed to be the most affected. She was wearing a blue dress—all stained with blood—that she refused to change despite the intervention of her friends. These relatives explained her sad story to us: the loyalist soldiers had entered her home, where they found her husband as well as the woman's four older boys. They grabbed them and led them out behind the house, where they slit their throats. The woman was later beaten and raped, as she had resisted the soldiers.

11

The journey to the 4th *arrondissement* took 45 minutes. When we arrived, we saw barriers being erected there that were controlled by these loyalist soldiers. We were immediately arrested and our bags were searched. This checkpoint was put in place to arrest all those who were of the Yaki ethnic group. Thus, there was a mandatory requirement to speak in patois—that is, everyone had to speak in the language of the ethnic group they claimed to belong to. The soldiers also checked the signs and various characteristics that typified each of the country's ethnic groups.

In the meantime, children and pregnant women were allowed to pass through. All men, on the contrary, were to be arrested and taken to the Karako base, where everyone had to prove they were not of the Yaki ethnic group. This was an organized and gruesome, bloodthirsty game, one from which all the horrors flowed. The arrested men were taken directly to the Karako base, where everything took place. This base was located upstream from the Ndress cemetery, a few metres from a small riverbank forest called 'Les Fleurs'. In this camp, there were a significant number of armed men. They were robust and ruthless. These men were on drugs all the time and had the visible appearance of monsters. Blood was spilled all over the ground, which was covered with decomposing human corpses. The base stank of death. Large swarms of flies hovered around these disfigured bodies. No one could identify the bodies.

There were graves one metre deep dug everywhere. Some of those arrested were buried alive.

We arrived in the camp and saw that a group of Yaki youths had been arrested. These Yaki youths were tied to trees, and tyres were also attached to them. Two men among the arrested Yaki were not tied up. They were subjected to the camp leader's questioning, in order to force them to give up their secrets or to give up their rebel families. They refused to answer the questions, and that cost them dearly. They were immediately passed on to different methods of torture that were in place. They were made to lie on the ground, where they were beaten with heavy weapons and clubs. The soldiers, wearing military boots, trampled on their heads. But these methods yielded no results either.

The loyalist leader found it useful to change tactics to increase their suffering and push them to their limits. He decided to cut small branches of trees and carefully prune the ends to the shape of an arrow. The two Yaki men, who until then had resisted, were seized again by five loyalist soldiers to undergo the new torture method. They were stretched out on the ground, and the chief of the Karako base came with these pieces of trees with cut ends. He inserted them into the anus of each of these Yaki. He pushed them in with all his strength, so that these branches could penetrate them deeply. From this, there could be no alternative but a violent and sudden death. These pieces of wood passed through their bellies and pierced their entrails. And, finally, these two Yaki

13

men struggled in vain against death. Blood came out of their mouths, their anuses, and even their ears.

The men's bound companions, who watched the torture helplessly, shouted hysterically as they sobbed. But there was no one or anything that could save them. Two other arrested men were untied, to put them through the same procedures. Faced with the agony and sufferings undergone, they found nothing better than to spit in the face of the base leader. Fear overwhelmed them. They were shaking and pissing themselves. They could feel that death was right there. Despite all this, they decided to stand up to the loyalist leader. So the latter decided to slightly modify his procedure. He had them put on the ground facing the sky. Instead of having the arrows pushed into their anuses, the leader decided that the arrows would be forced into their mouths. They forced in the arrows with blows of a hammer, such that they pierced the men's necks. A kind of white cream with blood came out of their brains. But that was not enough. They were cut into small pieces. Their heads were cut off first, then the other parts of their bodies.

Then the hateful-eyed commander turned to the other people tied to the trees and surrounded by tyres. He told them forcefully not to make the mistake of wasting his time. They should tell him everything he wanted to know; otherwise, their fate would be worse than that of the previous ones. However, they hurled abuse at him and also spat into his face. He became extremely angry and ordered that they be burned alive. His order was immediately carried out, and petrol was poured over their whole bodies and they were set on fire. The blaze began to consume them. They burned in agony, trying in vain to free themselves from their bonds. They screamed and rolled around in the huge inferno. The armed men encircled them and gleefully watched the scene. Those whose ropes were severed by the flames and who tried to get up to flee and escape the fire were gunned down. They all died, some from the heat of the fire and others from the shooting.

From most of the trees covering the base, human corpses were hanging in the air, with large flies landing on them. Arrested men were regularly brought in to be murdered. Karako base was indeed a place of doom, reeking of death. Everything there seemed to be grief-stricken, and the place was a perfect reflection of hell. Man became animalized, losing all sense of the value and dignity of the human person.

Chapter 3

After long periods of waiting, we had to pass through the roadblocks. And then we finally arrived in the 4th *arrondissement*. A completely different atmosphere reigned there. Its inhabitants, *a priori*, did not seem to be joyful about our arrival. Hatred and anger could be read in their eyes. They were hostile to this mass of displaced persons. We began to receive insults from all sides. The residents treated us like a bunch of cockroaches, murderers, and traitors. We had stones thrown at us and people spat into our faces. We were not accepted by these residents, who labelled us 'rebels'.

Night approached and we had to find a place to sleep, because the people would not let us go further. As a consequence, no displaced persons could get to their welcoming relatives. Also, it was difficult for the families to come and pick us up—because the families would be subjected to the same fate as us and be treated as accomplices or also as rebels. This complicated things, and there was nothing we could do about it. In addition, some of us had returned to their relatives, helped by the residents of goodwill who did not share the views of the general population there.

The mayor of the district appeared. He requested that they organize a reception centre at the municipal level. We were taken to a centre where tents were improvised. My friends and I did not find any tents, so we decided to spend the night on the bare ground in the moonlight.

Right at the entrance to the town hall, a crowd of young people who were hostile to our settlement were calling for our heads. They gathered under the trees located in front of the municipality. They somehow wanted us all to be killed, and the situation became more and more tense as the number of demonstrators progressively increased.

As a consequence, the mayor ordered the police, the loyalist police, to secure the premises and repel the demonstrators. A great fear seized us. Some children and women burst into tears. We had now become strangers and cockroaches in our own land, wandering hither and thither.

Night fell. The makeshift camp was covered in darkness. A few lamps and candles glowed in the middle of a gloomy atmosphere. A great silence reigned there, and no one could afford the luxury of going out of the camp. Under my sheet, I meditated on our fate and asked myself why there was so much hatred and division among us Central Africans—we who were in fact a single people. I saw that the whole camp was in prayer. I could hear from all sides the prayers, 'Our Father, who art in Heaven' and 'Hail Mary'. The children were clinging tightly to their mothers and did not understand much about this bizarre situation.

The police continued to mount a guard around the camp until at least 10 p.m. My friends and I decided to find a place in an old municipal bus, parked not far from the south exit. We spent the night under the bus, away from my mother and my younger sister.

Around one o'clock in the morning, loud cries were heard in the camp. I jumped up under the impact of the high-pitched sounds of a general panic. The camp was being attacked by assailants with machetes, who began to decapitate people. Those who tried to escape were shot. Women and children were sprawled on the ground dead. I slid discreetly under the bus, dragging behind me my other friends, who were already awake. We hid under the bus, unable to escape. The stampede and the spectacle were terrible to witness. Those who wanted to jump over the walls to save themselves were caught by the barbed wire, which scratched them badly. Also, some of these assailants simply waited behind the walls and picked off the fugitives at will.

All the residents of the periphery woke up and rushed to the town hall, where the cries and sounds of weapons were heard. In this cacophony, the police officers who were assigned there resurfaced, hypocritically trying to repel the assailants. These police officers were plainly in cahoots with the attackers. My friends and I could not hurry to come out from where we were hiding. We watched the situation unfold in great trepidation. The hypocritical intervention of the police officers was nevertheless beneficial, because a precarious calm returned.

A quarter of an hour later, a Red Cross ambulance appeared. The dead bodies were collected and piled up in this funeral device like pieces of wood. Also, the wounded were taken to the Hôpital de l'Amitié. My friends and I and other survivors of the carnage had finally come out of our dens, tingling with fear and grief. Had my mother and younger sister died in the assault? Yes, they had both died. We gathered to mourn our loved ones massacred during that dawn. I cried to the point when I wanted to kill myself. Losing my mother … what a shock! She was everything to me, a truly gentle and loving mother.

Given the severity of the situation, the mayor decided to organize shelter among volunteer families. This was intended to try to protect us from further massacres. The initiative was not in vain, because a large number of families welcomed us into their homes, in spite of the obstacles due to the resistance and hostility of certain sections of the population, who considered us to be 'invaders'.

A painful life was reserved for us because of the refusal of the other inhabitants to co-exist with us. I was welcomed into the Bougué family, which had a positive attitude toward the displaced. This family understood that we were victims of social divisions and ethnico-political clashes. I tried to adapt to this new situation. Every day, a member of this family took me criss-crossing the neighbourhoods to visit close relatives or friends.

One day, we decided to go to the market for some household shopping. Along the way, we came across a striking, cruel scenario: a group of children aged 10 to 11 years, who were playing football, threw themselves on another child who was one of the displaced and who had been welcomed into another family. They chased him and dragged him to the ground, calling him a cockroach, a dog. They stoned him half to death with large rocks. This really angered me and the family member who accompanied me. I drove them away and recovered the child.

However, in the shade, the parents of the children who were playing observed the scene, all excited without reacting. Seeing me behaving in this way, they pounced on me and beat me savagely with pieces of wood. I was stripped of the money I had been given for the market and they threw me into a small canal. The person that was with me ran to alert the family. My host family hastened to my aid and rushed me off to hospital.

The vicious attitude of the people of the 4th *arrondissement* did not soften. A project to exterminate our ethnic group was fomented by the regime in power. Whenever we went to the market to buy food, the sellers would immediately raise the price of commodities. Sometimes they refused to sell them to us. We were forced to huddle together and lived in constant fear.

How can we not think of plurality as an asset? It involves the acceptance and tolerance of others as well as of their habits; it is a rich and painless blend of our ethnic, cultural, and religious differences. And no leader can govern a people if he has not a sense of gathering together. No ethnic group can think it is superior to others such that it can subjugate them to its whims. Clanism, regionalism, and nepotism are the main factors in our misfortunes. Injustices, inequalities, and oppression can lead only to the decline of a nation. The greatest leader is the one who must think all, do all, and dare all for his people. He can never have a good night's sleep if his expectations are not largely met. He must give his life for his people, sacrificing himself for unity and their perfect integration into the process of national development. He is a faithful servant and not a savage despot.

On my sick bed, I turned events over in my mind to see things clearly. I could not arrive at an understanding of why others did not accept us. Beside me was a girl who was watching me. I asked her to summon a member of my host family. After about half an hour, Agbo, the mother of this foster family, arrived. She clasped me in her arms and cried without ceasing. So I expressed my disillusionment and my wish to return to my home *arrondissement*— because, I thought to myself, there was no reason why I should sacrifice my innocence for the sake of ridiculous political and ethnic divisions. Abgo was upset at the thought that I wanted to return to my *arrondissement*, which had become a site of massacres and appalling crimes.

Mama Agbo's pleas were in vain, despite the recourse she made to her husband when she brought him to persuade me to remain. I got out of bed and took my bags with me under the bewildered gaze of Agbo and her husband. The whole family loved me very much, and the children never wanted to separate from me.

Chapter 4

I started walking and walking, alone, crying and thinking about my mother, who had been killed during the attack by the assailants on the municipal centre. Refusing to pass through the Karako base again, I cut another way through the riverbank forest 'Les Fleurs' not far from this base. I went into the meadow to avoid the militias and discovered a newly marked trail, which seemed to come from the Karako base. This made me panic and, at the same time, evoked resistance in me— because there was no way I was going to turn back. I decided to continue straight ahead at my own risk and peril.

On the way, I heard people screaming and movements coming from my right in a small clump of grass. I approached carefully to find out what was going on. I discovered a group of loyalist militiamen raping women and their children. And they raped and tormented them with little resistance. Powerless in the face of such a situation, I simply continued on the road.

The loyalist militias abandoned their guard post and they all seemed to be attracted to this rape incident. Their weapons were abandoned on the ground, and they argued furiously over who should be next. In this atmosphere, the idea crossed my mind to pick up their abandoned weapons and kill them all. But I was far from the crime scene, and the slightest movement would alert them immediately. I also did not know how to use a gun. I decided to go straight back, skirting around the scene.

When I arrived in my *arrondissement*, the atmosphere was very bleak. Life and joy were no longer there. I rushed home to get news about my father. The front door was ajar and Papa was not there. I shouted: 'Papa, Papa'—but with no success. The house had been looted, and I saw debris from our stolen possessions on the ground. Immediately, I decided to go and see if he might be in the basement. He was not there either. I went out to ask the neighbours. They told me Papa had crossed to the other side of the Oubangui River, to Congo, to go into exile. So I remained alone, pondering, knowing that no one was there to help me.

Some people began to return to their respective homes, and life was quietly returning to normal. I tried to put the house in order, waiting for Papa to return. I tinkered with repairing the furniture and tried to prepare something to eat. But there was no longer any food in the house.

Later, I tried to find out how to get in touch with Papa to get news from him. However, I found nothing that could lead me to him. The only other option would be for me to also cross the Oubangui River to the refugee camp. But no one had returned from refuge, and the soldiers no longer allowed anyone to cross over. They said that people would feed the rebels or provide them with intelligence information. It could also cost me my life.

After this failed coup d'état, President Kota became increasingly enraged and cruel, instituting drastic security measures to stifle and restrict the rights and public freedoms of individuals. Police misdeeds were added to this daily. One could observe all the time cases of kidnapping and secret disappearances of people close to the opposition or the Yaki ethnic group. A regime of terror took hold, and people's living conditions worsened. People began to grind their teeth and no longer dared to hope for a bright future. The regime became increasingly unbearable; only the clans close to power could live in luxury and roam freely in the country. In addition, there was an increase in rebellions in the provinces, which decided to overthrow Kota in order to establish a more democratic regime. And this was the hope of the forgotten, the marginalized. Thus, rebel groups became increasingly active and advanced slowly toward the capital, Bangui.

Chapter 5

It was very dark outside, and not a soul passed along the streets. Papa had had nothing to eat after a week of military manhunts and abuses. He decided to leave his cubbyhole ... to go somewhere. He was wet with sweat due to the lack of ventilation in the basement.

Outside, he walked down the small alleyway that led to the Church of St. Paul. He decided to go to the port of Sao to cross to Zongo. When he arrived at the Oubangui River, he saw on the other shore a group of Congolese fishermen who were staying up and checking their nets at night. Papa called to ask them to come to help him. All were reluctant to rescue someone who had come out of nowhere, who could be an impostor in the pay of the Central African border police.

But knowing the latest escapades of this 'ghost' state and the recent spectacular nocturnal crossings of a segment of the Central African population, they agreed to come closer, asking him why he was calling to them.

There were three fishermen, and two of them spoke Sango fluently since their town is about 15 minutes away from Zongo–Bangui. Papa negotiated that he would be taken across to the Congo refugee camp. For this, they demanded a sum of 15,000 CFA francs. He begged them and agreed to give them 5,000 francs. That same night, they crossed the river and landed on the other side, on the Congolese shore.

It was one o'clock in the morning, and Papa could go no further except to sleep by the riverside, waiting for the sunrise.

His hosts had him lie down near their bags; they re-lit their abandoned fire to grill fish taken from their nets. The fish was lightly grilled with oil and salt. Papa shared this meal with them and chatted about the crisis in his country. After a while, his friends left him to continue their work. Alone and thoughtful, Papa could not get to sleep. He was worried about our separation, about what might happen, as he had had no news of us. With his eyes fixed on the sky, he contemplated the twinkling stars, tossing and turning in all directions without sleeping.

At 4 a.m., the roosters crowed and announced the day. Other fishermen flocked to the river. Papa struggled against a feeling of sluggishness, but eventually he got up. He walked along the river and observed the activities of the local residents. After half an hour, his friends returned to him. Papa was obsessed by the idea of finding the refugee camp, but the fishermen advised him to remain patient and wait until 7:30 or 8:00 a.m., the opening time of the administrative posts.

The fishermen packed their bags around 5 a.m. and left the river for their respective homes. In the meantime, one of the fishermen had suggested that my father go to his house before he was taken to the UNHCR.

When he arrived, Papa sat in an old armchair on the veranda, where he could see a ramshackle house, blackened with smoke, that was used to dry the caught fish. The air smelled of rotten fish, those which had not been bought. Papa concentrated on waiting until the time indicated, to go to the UNHCR.

His fisherman friend came out of the house, where he had been for a while, and his wife afterward; she was getting ready to prepare the fire for breakfast and sweep the yard. She politely whispered a little '*Mboté*' hello, with a smiling face. Papa said hello and smiled back to her, introducing himself at the same time.

It seems that Papa was not the only one to pass through this family. During this period, so many other Central Africans had also passed through before going on to the UNHCR. It was, in a way, a transit house or a temporary refuge for refugees, because of this fisherman's connection with the river.

At 8:00 a.m. Papa was driven to the UNHCR office. He was exposed to a pile of questionnaires from the UNHCR Department of International Protection. He gave his identity: Papa was a colonel in the national army, close to the earlier deposed president, Sokpa. He had worked for and been very supportive of the fallen regime. And for him, this change in the country was a great shock.

His identity placed him in the ranks of political refugees. For this reason, he had to go to the camp maintained for military refugees, which was carefully guarded by the Congolese armed forces, FARDC. The camp was more than 15 km from Zongo, separate from the civilian refugee camp.

Papa met his old friends at the refugee camp, most of them close to the Yaki ethnic group. So they started talking about the failed coup d'état, about everything and nothing. They asked him if his family was doing well. He replied that he had heard no news of us since our departure for the 4th *arrondissement*.

At the entrance to the camp, FARDC maintained the peace. They continually inspected the site and kept an eye on everyone. Papa and the others began to review what had happened, why the coup d'état had failed. They blamed the overall coordination of operations and denounced the leader of the coup d'état, who had not given them all the means necessary for its success.

The Yaki soldiers wanted to return to office after ten years in power. They believed in creating a dynasty that would last forever in time and space. But nature had decided otherwise: the first democratic elections in 1993 gave victory to Kota, and all that dynastic order collapsed. A new era began. A new regime, a new team; a new class of friends and girlfriends and concubines, a new village invested with power. And everything that had existed had been swept away.

So this situation did not suit our power-hungry Yaki parents. They orchestrated one mutiny after another, in order to remove the established regime. Being in exile had no effect on their desire to return to power. In the refugee site, they regularly deliberated over how to mount a new coup d'état.

Radio announcements were broadcast on the airwaves, requesting all deserting soldiers to return to their respective barracks or they would be discharged from the army; this was especially relevant to the soldiers who had been involved in the failed coup d'état.

Papa had no excuses to offer, and the desire to find his family haunted him.

However, this news did not please everyone; many other deserters decided to remain in exile to continue their struggle. They wanted to mount a larger rebellion to overthrow Kota. All of my father's friends were planning the future in this direction: returning to occupy high positions of responsibility, advancing in rank. Some were already thinking of the Ministry of Defence, of the Interior, and of Public Security, as well as the Army General Staff.

As a result, Papa contemplated his escape, in order to return to the country. In the meantime, FARDC continued to behave well up to a given point; then they let the refugees out in exchange for bribes. The refugees went down to Zongo to entertain themselves in the bistros on the square, accompanied by young Congolese girls who worshipped the CFA franc.

Papa, who until then had kept his distance from these activities, found no other way to escape. Taking the same path and going to Zongo on a Saturday evening with some of his colleagues, he went into a bistro with them and ordered beer and *yabanda*[8] made with smoked fish ....

Papa was wearing faded jeans and a dark-blue t-shirt and sported a pair of Nike shoes. He was a tall, strong, and muscular man, measuring 1.80 m. He liked stylish and beautiful women.

In the bistro where they were, there were also young Congolese girls who were competing in the game 'chasing after the men'. All of them were watching the newcomers.

The music playing was 'Apologize' by Timbaland, a black American. My father went up to the dance floor to dance. He danced light, circular dance steps, accentuated by overall movements. With his arms out horizontally and his head raised, he danced two steps forward, one back, controlled by the rhythmic pulse. Immediately, the Congolese women swarmed onto the dance floor; they were obviously flirting with these soldiers. They gradually moved closer and closer to my father, who until then had been alone on the dance floor.

Carried along by the charms of these young Congolese girls between 16 and 22 years old, Papa had to make a choice. He scrutinized them with a sharp gaze, focusing on form and beauty. He made his choice: a slim Sèpêlè girl of coffee-with-milk colour and a beautiful figure, 1.70 m tall, whom he invited to dance. With this development, the DJ

---

[8] *Yabanda:* a generic term for a dish of stewed vine leaves (called *koko* in Sango, *gnetum* in French), to which one can add smoked fish or caterpillars.

31

changed the music and slipped deliciously into 'Rumba Congolaise', 'Ikéa', and 'BB Gôut'—tracks from the artist Koffi Olomidé.

My father's other friends followed him onto the dance floor, and each of these girls managed to get her man. Music and beer enlivened the atmosphere.

The evening wound up in the motels on the square, where everything came to completion ....

Using his girlfriend Doris's telephone that same night around 10 p.m., my father called his fisherman friend, who came to pick him up an hour later. They both returned to the riverbank; his friend did his best and organized my father's return to Bangui.

Chapter 6

I slept deeply on piles of cardboard that were lying on the bare ground, after a long day of games and chatting with the neighbours' children. I took refuge in these games, to forget the burden of life, my suffering, and the loneliness that crushed me. Often I would eat at the neighbours' houses or go fishing with their children to catch small fish in the streams that flow into the Oubangui River, in order to have something to eat. Also, I went to the house of my grandmother, who regularly provided me with small supplies of rice, oil, sugar, beans, and so on.

Around 4 a.m., Papa entered the house; he looked at the small body asleep alone in the cool of the dawn. He could not wake me up. He scoured the house with his eyes and found no one else. He saw that everything had been stolen, even the electric cables. He leaned against the wall and tried to account for the absence of the others. Where were they gone? He said to himself that Mama and my sister would be at grandmother's house. But this hypothesis did not add up, because Mama could not leave me alone in the house. His eyes reddened as soon as his explanation failed to make sense. Nevertheless, he let me continue my sleep.

When I woke up at 6 a.m., I found him sitting on the floor with his back stuck against the wall. At that moment, he ran to enfold me in his arms, with large tears running down from his eyes. He immediately asked me:

'Where are the others?'

I also burst into tears, replying sorrowfully:

'Mama is dead, and Audrey is with grandmother.'

I had the impression that everything was spinning around us. Papa fell over onto the ground and wept loudly. I had never seen him in such a state before. His sorrow was profound! It is difficult to describe the scene. He blamed himself for abandoning us. He scarcely believed that I could bear all this and sleep alone in such a large house. He observed me silently, wishing to make sure I was alright.

The day was dawning. Papa sent me to fetch water for him for washing and breakfast; he could not go outside for fear of being seen by people who would go to betray him to the police and security forces. He forbid me to tell anyone about his arrival. He washed, and we ate breakfast in silence. We set about fixing up and cleaning the house. We spent the whole day around questions that we asked each other as well as around little tales of our adventures. We ate some restaurant food at lunchtime and took our afternoon nap together in my parents' room.

At 6 p.m., he decided to walk over to my grandmother's house. I wanted to go with him, but he refused so as not to take too long getting there. When he arrived, he found my grandmother, my little sister, and some of our uncles in conversation in the living room. His entry upset everyone and the atmosphere changed immediately. My grandmother accused him of having murdered her daughter and abandoning her grandchildren to her. Papa had no words to console her or to express the shock that my mother's death had caused him. He let himself be stung by the reproaches and insults of my uncles. He apologized and explained why he had let us go to the 4th *arrondissement*.

In the end, Papa told my grandmother to take care of my sister, as he had to go to his base for the announced inspection. My uncles as well as my grandmother forbade him to do so, because of the torture, abductions, and murders suffered by deserters. But he replied that he could not stay in hiding forever ....

Papa came home and told me his decision. I heaved a heavy sigh and sat down in anger. So he took pains to explain his decision to me. He told me that if he did not do it, he would be arrested and his situation would become even more complicated. He gave me some money and took me up in his arms. He assured me that he would come back and that everything would return to normal. He set me down, entered his room, and told me to be careful. Also, he proposed that I go to get news of him at his battalion if it turned out that he did not return home soon. If anything were to happen to him, he urged me to go back to my grandmother and let one of my uncles occupy the house after him.

The night he announced this decision to me I was completely despondent. How could he again abandon us? I also went to bed. A small lamp lit the room and showed no sign of life. On the mat that served as my bed, I curled up under an old sheet and started crying again. From his room, Papa heard my sobbing and came to sleep with me. He did his best to console me, telling me about the trials of life before which we must not submit. I was able to comfort myself because I wished to avoided hurting him more.

The next morning, he left for his base. Once he arrived, he had himself registered and he explained to his superiors why he had deserted. His reason was that all former military guards close to the deposed president, Sokpa, were automatically targeted, even if they did not all take part in the failed coup d'état—so he could not risk his life by staying in the country.

This argument did not convince them. He would not have feared for his life, the authorities retorted, if he had done nothing wrong. Why flee the country for three months following the coup d'état and hope to justify his action by fear of being hunted because of his ethnicity and his rapprochement with the regime? This position was not really the best one for my father, who found himself there with other returned deserters. He was arrested on the spot, imprisoned at his base, and they reported the information to the Army General Staff. The General Staff decided to send him to a prison kept secret for these cases—an intolerable place.

As soon as he entered the prison, Papa saw the inhuman and degrading conditions of detention. A fellow inmate sitting right next to the front door welcomed him ironically: he put his hand in his nose in a gesture of avoiding foul odours. But this was not all; Papa vomited and sweated heavily.

In addition, another fellow prisoner pointed out to him that people were abducted there at night and at any hour every night; and everyone armed themselves so that this fate would not befall them. Obsessive fear seized hold of everyone, and life oscillated between fear and death.

Papa shook his head negatively and sat against the wall of a small, almost rectangular room, which served as a cubicle and contained more than five people. Sixty centimetres from where he was sitting there was a hole full of excrement and vomit, on which were crawling cockroaches, flies, maggots, and bugs, and which stank badly. At the sight of all this, Papa wanted to cough up his innards, but he had to keep his spirits up in this situation. The food was shared three times a week—inedible, disgusting meals.

That same night when Papa entered the prison, a man was abducted. When the guards dragged him outside, he cried like a fat sow and woke up the whole prison. He begged the guards in vain, pleading in sorrow: 'Don't kill me; my children need me. I beg you; let go of me ....'

Papa lost all courage, all hope; his morale was low and he bitterly regretted his choice to voluntarily surrender.

No one could learn the fate of this abducted man afterward. Sometimes, prisoners wanted to commit suicide in the face of the sufferings—an idea that also crossed my father's mind that night: to renounce life, to commit suicide. He was sick of everything and regretted joining the army. He said to himself that this Central African nation is a social disaster, a hell.

Alas, this nation was adrift. To favour nepotism and ethnico-political divisions as a tool for governing a nation—this is like a land perched on a volcano. And when the elite of the state are pervaded by a lack of revolutionary fervour, the narrow-minded people who compose this elite delight in the pursuit of a decadence whose victim is the population.

Chapter 7

I was bored at home! Loneliness haunted me and I was restless all the time. After two weeks, I decided to go to the Camp Béal base where my father had gone, to get news of him. A lady in the secretariat who knew my father told me that he was no longer at the camp but had been transferred to a place of detention for soldiers, a place where access was strictly forbidden to unauthorized persons. However, she reassured me that my father was fine.

On my way out, she slipped me a piece of paper with the name and number of a staff sergeant, Bonafi, assigned to this prison; she whispered in my ear that this man could help me to get news of my father. She also told me where to go to meet this sergeant.

I went the next day to the place indicated. Only soldiers passed through there, and the area was very quiet. A few metres away, soldiers were on sentry duty and were seriously involved in guarding. From a distance, one of them gestured to me with her hand to leave the place and go away; but this did not frighten me. I took small steps in her direction, assuming an air of being justified in doing so. She let me come closer to her and asked me what I was looking for. I told her I was looking for Staff Sergeant Bonafi. Would I say why? I did not answer her. She continued:

'Is he your father?'

I answered her in the affirmative.

She pointed me to a checkpoint. I went there and asked for Staff Sergeant Bonafi. He jumped up and looked at me with a grumpy look on his face, wondering did we know each other.

'What brings you here?', he said to me.

I told him that I had come looking for news of my father, Colonel Yambi.

'And who gave you my name?'

I remained silent and lowered my head, to avoid his menacing gaze. A rude woman who was listening to us said to me:

'Little man, this is not a hospital for you to stroll around in.'

Staff Sergeant Bonafi scratched his head, then pulled me with him into a corner a little to one side. He scolded me and asked me why I was taking such a risk.

'Access here is forbidden, son.'

I told him I had come to get news of my father. He told me that my father was his trainer and that he had great respect for him, but that this situation in which Papa found himself was beyond his reach. He said to me:

'This place is hell; only the power or the current regime can decide on the life or death of someone. There's no justice for the weak; everything is corrupted, influenced by power. Decisions, therefore, cannot be changed.'

So he told me that he could not promise me anything, but that he would try to do something to help my father.

Tears were running down my face and I was distraught. He took my hand and led me to the exit.

'You're very brave and I'm proud of you. You're really doing something that is above your age.' He kissed me, gave me some money, and told me to go home.

I returned home with a lot of questions. What would happen to my father? If they killed him, what would become of us? The picture I formed in mind was all black. If Papa would no longer be there, we would have to go to sleep with our grandmother, or with our maternal uncles.

I went into the room and cried, because my father's situation could get worse. During this time, I needed my mother—to support me, to comfort me—but she was no longer there. In front of me was a black void.

The next day, I went to my grandmother's house to explain about my father's situation. Some of my uncles were there; they agreed to work together to rescue my father. In the meantime, I gave them the number of the sergeant who had spoken to me and told me that the Chief of the Defence Staff was my father's comrade-in-arms. The man in question, General Mafouta, knew my father very well, according to the sergeant.

They called the sergeant at home on the phone and wanted him to put them in touch with the Chief of the Defence Staff. My uncles and grandmother wanted to go and meet the Chief of the Defence Staff. But Staff Sergeant Bonafi advised us against going to the Chief of the Defence Staff right away. He would go first to his house and then tell us what we could do afterward—because, according to the staff sergeant, he was a close relative of the Chief of the Defence Staff.

This development really excited us; we wanted to do our best to free Papa. On a Saturday afternoon, the staff sergeant went to General Mafouta's house. He explained to him the situation of my father, his comrade-in-arms. The general informed him that he was aware of his situation and was thinking about how to help him. In this regard, he told the staff sergeant that he was negotiating the release of my father with the President of the Republic. We were really in suspense at the development of this situation; we waited and hoped against all hope for my father's release.

One night, my father was grabbed by two prison guards, who dragged him outside. He believed that day that everything was over for him; he was going to die like the others. His prison friends lamented for him, believing that my father would be murdered. My father begged these guards not to take away his life, because he had children who needed him. He was shaking and agitated, hoping to find a way of deliverance, of salvation. These guards told him:

'Don't be afraid of anything, Colonel. We're not going to harm you. General Mafouta needs you.'

At these words, my father calmed down. He heaved a deep sigh. They made him change his clothes and took him in a jeep. They entered the general's compound at around 9 p.m. and Papa immediately recognized the place; it was indeed the general's house. They made him sit in the general's straw hut, accompanied by two other guards who replaced the first ones—the replacements were the general's own bodyguards.

After about 15 minutes, the general appeared. He greeted my father in a friendly manner and told him to sit down. He ordered his bodyguards to leave them alone. The general entered directly into conversation and began by asking for news of Papa's family. General Mafouta recalled the intrigues of the Yaki soldiers and especially my father's involvement in such a story. He strongly reproached him for this, saying that an enlightened person could not be influenced by ethnic, racist ideologies that were designed to destabilize the country. He laid out for him the unfortunate consequences which were also reserved for Papa. He told him about the intervention of Staff Sergeant Bonafi, who had asked for his release. Also, the ties that united them since they had joined the army. Papa remained riveted to the chair, his mouth hanging open, aware of the unpatriotic panurgism in which he had immersed himself. The general told him that he was free, but that he should not leave the country or have contact with other rebel soldiers ….

What makes the Central African man stupid and ridiculous is that he easily joins forces with foreign powers to destroy his country. The five decades of crisis we have experienced proves how stupid we are, easily manipulated and unable to use our heads to solve our problems. Central Africa has never had a political leader who sacrificed himself for this nation—except perhaps the founding president, who was prematurely assassinated.

The greatest crime against humanity is to create from a nation a heritage whose subjects and wealth are enslaved to the desires of a handful of crude, corrupt, criminal, and savage individuals. Everything that does not serve the common interest can never last in the face of the tests of time; nepotism, clanism, regionalism, and so on can never hold up against the will of the dreaming masses, eager for a better future ….

Chapter 8

My father's release was a great relief for the whole family. Papa came home and picked us up at our grandmother's house. On the first day, we observed a few minutes of silence at the place where our mother had died. After that, Papa tried and wished us to start afresh, to turn over a new page on the past. But how could we easily forget the past that had engulfed our mother? We were more attached to Mama than to him. And, from time to time, he spent days elsewhere on account of work activities ....

Meanwhile, he also had other children from his first relationship, with Agate, from whom he had separated after meeting my mother. Our mother and we knew very well that he spent his time philandering, so he lied to us.

A few months later, Papa was reinstated in his position with the support of the Chief of the Defence Staff. But this news displeased his fellow deserters who had remained in hiding. They called him a traitor, a chicken. However, my father wanted to be close to his family and resume a normal life. He was fed up with a hidden life, a life of exile, given his rank as a colonel, an officer of the state. We thus little by little regained control of our lives.

When our father went back to work, my sister and I noticed after a while that he was less regularly at home; he had reconnected with his ex-girlfriend, with whom he had had other children. He would leave us money for food and spend every other night away from home. We asked him how he could do that, turn his back easily on what happened to our mother? He fudged his answers, sometimes dodging the question.

The other deserters who remained in exile had not changed their perspective in any way. They gradually left the refugee camp and returned to the north of Central Africa, where they formed a strong rebellion called Zakawa, the 'liberators'. Some of them remained in Congo as the vanguard of all destabilization movements in the country.

This rebellion was supported by certain foreign powers hostile to the current regime. On 21 September 2001, a military offensive was again launched to depose Kota. It was led largely by the remaining team of deserters in Congo, as well as another part from the north that had stealthily infiltrated Bangui.

The militias from Zongo and those from some of the provinces took control of the national radio station and certain parts of Bangui city. The whole city was in panic, while President Kota was pinned down at his residence, where all his personal guards and loyalist soldiers were entrenched.

My father was in Petevo that day, a neighbourhood captured by rebel militias. And it so happened that colleagues he had released were advancing on that side in a heavily armed attack. Thus, my father, who was in this area, tried to leave as quickly as possible. He could not go directly down to the city centre, where the rebels had taken control of the national radio station. He therefore went up to the slaughterhouse located near the Oubangui River, to reach a port not far from the area. He again had the reflex to flee and return to the Congo.

Disaster! He fell into the hands of the rebel militias who occupied the entire length of the river; those he had abandoned seized him furiously and started to interrogate him:

'Where are you going?'

'I'm going to Zongo.'

'To Zongo, where you abandoned us, you dirty traitor?'

They made him kneel on the spot and beat him with their rifle butts. Papa was bleeding and his face was disfigured by these blows. They argued about whether to kill him or let him go.

Surprisingly, they found him a pirogue docked at the small port, from which he embarked. They let him pass. Papa rowed with all his strength, sweating and sighing deeply, trying to save his life. But when he arrived in the middle of the river, a gunshot rang out; he had just been shot. He dropped his oar and fell into the river. He drowned, submerged in the water ....

The loyalist forces managed to repel the rebel militias and regained control of the city and the radio station. The coup d'état failed once again, thanks to the support of Congolese mercenaries called Banyamoulengué, who came to support Kota.

The news of my father's death arrived at our stepmother's house a few days later. She went to comb all along the riverbank, looking for the body. She spent three days without finding the body. This did not discourage her; she extended the area of her search, further downstream, to the south of Bangui.

It turned out that the body was recovered by a fisherman, whose net had caught it. The fisherman removed the body from his net and buried it with the help of his crewmates, right on the bank of river—in a grave less than a metre deep, as the body had decomposed. The only clues provided by the fishermen—clothing, shoes, bracelet—identified the body and reassured my stepmother.

I was informed of the death of my father afterward by my grandmother, who long before the news of my father's death had picked up my sister. She was afraid that I might have a breakdown, sink into misery. I remained glued to the wall, crushed by sobbing. Everything was over for me; I had no reason to live ....

My grandmother understood my suffering; she took me in her arms without saying a word. She let me empty myself of my tears and, finally, she began to comfort me. Then she decided to take me with her. I refused her offer, deciding to take care of the belongings of my disappeared parents. She had never liked my rebellious attitude, the things I did from my own will. Even though life had just ripped away all those who were dear to us, and we would henceforth have to rely on the affection of our extended family to make up for the lack of parental affection—indispensable as it is for our self-development—still, I was more interested in what was real, because our biological parents can never be replaced.

Chapter 9

The group of armed gangs from neighbouring Congo lent a strong hand to Kota to save him from his perilous situation—because the rebels who resumed activities in the north of the country and who planned to come and take the capital were stopped and they turned back. President Kota gave the Banyamoulengué all the power and resources they needed to stop the advance of the rebels. As a result, they were placed at the head of the regiments and intervention brigades, thus relegating the loyalist soldiers to second place. From then on, the loyalists were to be used only to locate enemies. All fighting from now on would be controlled and commanded by the Banyamoulengué.

This new situation gave Kota the advantage, and he pushed the rebels back into the distance. However, the privileges and power granted to the Banyamoulengué made them undeniable masters, demigods. They marched on the provincial cities as formidable warriors, and their standing rarely inspired them with pity. They were cruel men, dealers in death; in their passage, they wallowed in violence and massacre. They were accountable to no one and imposed dictates on the submissive population. How could this be? The shame of a mediocre nation, insane. A nation that had long been run only by narrow-minded rulers.

The city of Bangui was overrun in the same way as the provincial cities. I lived in this bleak atmosphere, with no future. I had to go out on the street every day to get my daily bread. At one point, I could no longer walk outside because of the upheavals of the Banyamoulengué, who killed, raped, and looted incessantly. They also recruited children and some adults whether these people liked it or not. I understood that my life was more than ever in danger. I hid in the house, without food or anyone to talk to. I was sick of my life, which seemed to have capsized into a dream, while I swam in a life-reality without precedent—to the point where I preferred death to life. Hunger tortured me, and I could not remain hidden at home with nothing to eat.

I plucked up my courage and inched my way into the capital's neighbourhoods, observing the active Banyamoulengué patrols, which had erected barriers everywhere. When I wanted to take the street which followed the main avenue, I saw a group of Banyamoulengué militia who gathered six people, including a woman and a girl at least 14 years old, at the foot of a large teak tree. They were arguing over the woman and the girl. Four men that had been arrested with this woman and this girl were opposed to the Banyamoulengué's intentions to have forced sex with them. This opposition cost the men their lives, because these Banyamoulengué militiamen could not find anything better to do than to shoot them. After that, the Banyamoulengué seized and raped this woman and the girl.

The girl seemed to faint. She was losing a lot of blood from her genitals and cried without cease. And there was no one there to save her. I quickly withdrew from where I was watching the scene, to slip into the central market to gather some products abandoned by the merchants.

I saw that the Banyamoulengué militias were also there. Some were on duty to secure the perimeter of the market, while others looted the large shops in the square. They emptied these places of their goods and immediately had them loaded into army vehicles that had been entrusted to them. The products they looted included—among other things—laptop computers, refrigerators, motorcycles, bags of rice and sugar, oil, kilos of meat, household appliances.

I turned back, trying to return home. I staggered under the effect of hunger and exhaustion. That day the sun did not shine; everything was dismal. I saw the Banyamoulengué present throughout the city, mainly engaged in looting and raping women as well as children. I noticed that these vehicles loaded with plunder were automatically heading for the large port upstream, to embark in the direction of Congo.

I could not understand why the government did not react to the savage and barbaric acts perpetrated by the Banyamoulengué. Is this really a good way for Kota to treat his people? He delivered us to the barbarism of strangers; our mothers and sisters were raped before our eyes, for the sole purpose of saving his power. Therefore, he could kill everyone—but the most important thing would be that his comfortable position was preserved. Kota had no consideration for the people who were massacred on a daily basis.

The country became ungovernable. All the national defence forces were confined to their barracks. I walked around, pondering as I saw the mounting cruelty. Among the ranks of the loyalist forces, Kota gradually lost their support. The loyalists began to understand the grave mistake they had made in slaughtering the people in order to save a corrupt regime. They lined up behind the civilian population to stop the massacres by the Banyamoulengué, because the latter no longer made any distinction between ethnic groups or between loyalist or rebel militias. They were shooting at everything that was in front of them. Thus, the loyalists interposed themselves between the Banyamoulengué and the population. But they could not resist long enough, because they were seriously lacking the means of combat; and what they had was much less than the combat means of the Banyamoulengué.

Kota decided that the loyalist deserters, who joined either the rebels or the people, were also to be eliminated. And this order issued by Kota made the situation worse, because it became difficult for the Banyamoulengué to draw a distinction between sides. In a battle between the loyalists and the Banyamoulengué, the whole city was put to flight because of the heavy Banyamoulengué retaliation. The loyalists and some of the city's inhabitants fled and took refuge on the Gbazoubangui hill. I also joined the loyalist group, as I was surprised by the situation. We spent the night on the hill. There, we discovered a large pit filled with corpses that stank to high heaven. Hundreds of bodies were discovered. These bodies were those of the loyalist soldiers and certain persons close to the opposition—whom Kota discreetly eliminated at the hands of the Banyamoulengué, but especially at the hands of his close guards. As a result, my new friends and I could no longer remain on the hill. We had to leave the place as soon as possible.

Captain Neya, one of the resistant loyalists, organized our departure from the site. He thought that he and other loyalists should not keep their military uniforms on, for fear of being spotted outside the hill. They took care to get rid of the uniforms, putting on civilian clothes. They hid the uniforms in a hole they dug. Neya led us to the exit from the hill. Then, as we took a few steps toward the exit, a sudden attack by the Banyamoulengué surrounded us all. We were attacked and trapped by Banyamoulengué who had surrounded the place. They knew that we had taken refuge there in that hill. Our fate was sealed. No one could escape. Death was there. So they killed Neya and all his companions except for me, since I was obviously a child.

I was loaded into the Banyamoulengué's vehicle. They took me to the city centre, where they set up their base. I thus became a child soldier. I was given a dirty military outfit, larger than my size. I put it on without resisting. After that, I did not really know what was going to happen.

A lieutenant from the Banyamoulengué said I had to suffer the first hazing; and for this purpose, they organized my baptism of fire. They began by injecting me with drugs. A large fire was improvised. I was pushed into the middle of the fire, where I was beaten by rifle butts and belts. Live ammunition shots overwhelmed the city. It was supposed to take away my fear. Under the influence of these gunshots, I pissed in my clothes and was shaking, terrified. The other child soldiers mocked me and called me a weakling. A high dose of drugs was again administered to me. It made my head spin, and I fainted as I could not handle the dose. I fell down on the ground.

The sound of the weapons grew louder and louder, so the whole population was frightened. After that, they had to determine if I was ready for the front. So I had to submit to an ordeal by blood. I had to learn to kill, to kill without hesitation. A new lifestyle was imposed on me. Who was I supposed to kill? My fellow Central Africans, certainly: innocent women, children, and men. The life of Central African people had toppled into evil. We wallowed in total impunity.

After my baptism, I was driven to the Lakouanga district for my first test. We made our way into a house of seven people. The husband, wife, and children of the house were there. Lieutenant Moutoume said they were mine and that I should kill them all. Before that, they seized the woman and her two daughters, whom they raped. I was told to start with the husband and then his three boys. I spread them out on the floor to shoot them, when the lieutenant stopped me and told me not to proceed in that way. He pulled out his knife and passed it to me, saying I should cut off their heads. They had me tie them up. I put the knife to the father's throat. I held his head and started slitting his throat. He was much stronger than me. He struggled so forcefully that I had trouble cutting off his head. But I got the others to help me by grabbing him to make my task easier. So I cut off his head. His head fell under my feet and rolled on the floor. It horrified me and made me recoil, startled.

The heads of the man's other two children were also cut off. And as for the last boy, I had to tear his heart out. So I had to cut open his abdomen. I took the knife, trying to cut him open. I was unable to do so because I lacked the courage, seeing the results of the first actions. The task was entrusted to another young child soldier, who carried it out without any trouble. Thus, I understood what this new life was for me and that I had to find a way to get free from it.

All this gradually turned me into a monster. I became more active in the group and started to travel around the cities with them. I saw that many crimes were being committed. We arrived in a provincial town not far from the capital. There was a Catholic church there. We were ordered to seize the priests and tie them up. The lieutenant again appointed me to kill these unfortunate people. So I was handed a 5-litre can of petrol, which I poured over them. They were burned to death, and those who tried to escape were shot.

We were ordered to loot this locality. The order was followed, but I did not always agree with the others on their crimes. One day, I had a fierce fight with a young man, who ripped out the heart of a little girl whom he had first raped. I was punished for being opposed to this. I was put in the bottom of a dark pit, where I spent two days as a young man. I rebelled and began to be disgusted with this life. But there was no way for me to escape from it, because I was being watched.

I was not the only one who was enlisted. There were other children who had all become slaves to drugs. They obeyed the leaders like dogs and no longer knew their left from their right. They no longer had any notion of pity or emotion. Their lives became meaningless. We could easily be killed in an ambush or a strong attack by another rebel fringe.

I could not understand why the people of my country were subjected to all these sorrows. Nor could I accept the violence. No one believed in life any longer; the villagers cowered in the bush and lived on bark and wild leaves.

Interlude I: Tribute to African childhood

Oh black child, child of the world
Child of creative diversity
Your skin is not the product of a curse
Your skin has its origin in the Creative
Intelligence
Your skin is immutable, a matrix of
unfathomable richness
Your troubles, your sorrows, your pains, your
illnesses
Do not come from your skin at all
Your sorrows come from the mind, from the
soul
Of your saboteur ancestors
Whose existential inequalities
Made them slaves
Forced them into servitude
With cruelty and wickedness
Led them to servitude
Know that your ancestors were sleepers
Not knowing how to use the potential gifts of
nature
To be equal to all at the dawn of science
They were simply subjected to servitude
Because they were dreamers, innocent of the
infamous invasion
Millions of your decent, deported ancestors
Into the field of the humiliation of slavery
Exterminated by the pains of abomination

And loss, and shame, and misfortune, and crime
...
The next generations do not measure at all the
great gulf
To be filled between the two worlds
The new generations are not united in solidarity
To work toward the emergence of their land
They are, oh black child, your corrupt leaders
Thieves who are keeping you
In mediocrity, in poverty
An Africa that dies on the waves of immigration
An Africa that prostitutes itself
Uprooting itself on the grounds of
interdependence
She lacks the resourcefulness to match them
Oh black child, don't let it get you down
By the incessant sounds of war
They will have an end
And a new dawn will emerge
Oh black child, if you listen to me now
Lay down the weapons of your heart, of your
mind
From your hands and go back on the path
Of school, of wisdom, of fulfilment
Naturally, a child is a treasure
If he is well treated
Because he is called to the inheritance
To serve his society, his continent
The images we have of you
Show how much you are in need
Of tremendous help, support

To equal the other children on the planet
Here's a proverb:
'A family, a nation without children
Is destined to disappear'
Oh black child,
Don't think you're being abandoned
For many hearts full of
Good will are groaning
To see you happy and prosperous
Oh Central African child,
Be united forever
Reconcile yourself with your past history
Move forward and grow
In national cohesion
For the love of your country

Chapter 10

People began to repel the actions of the Banyamoulengué. In this way, resistance was organized. All over, Banyamoulengué vehicles were subjected to deadly ambushes. The inhabitants took their revenge. Everything was shaken up again. People began to come out of the bush.

A fringe of loyalist militias returned to the bush for rebellion. A large number of unemployed young people, along with people of all ages, decided to join the rebellion to return to overthrow Kota. This rebellion became significant as the number of people increased.

The Banyamoulengué were lynched everywhere by the population. They began to flee the violence and return to the Congo. This rebellion, led by Boté, which was joined by a large number of loyalist soldiers, regained control of all the provinces and prepared a major assault on Bangui. These rebels were called liberators, Zakaya. They were Central Africans and Chadians. Boté had gone to ask for Chad's support to overthrow Kota and the Banyamoulengué. These Chadian mercenaries were merciless, never backing down in the face of death. Without them, neither the Boté rebellion nor the loyalist soldiers could stand up to the Banyamoulengué machine. This was the first massive entry of Chadian mercenaries into the country. Loyalist militias led by Chadian mercenaries attacked the Banyamoulengué savagely. Everywhere, the population also rained down on them and beheaded them. Often, they were hacked into small pieces and even thrown into crocodile boxes.

This vengeance was not the half of it. We saw, all over the capital, Banyamoulengué heads cut off and hung up by young people, especially by the motorcycle taxi drivers. I took advantage of this uncontrolled situation to escape, abandoning the ranks of the Banyamoulengué when we had taken refuge in the capital because of the rebels' advance with Chadian support. In this way, I returned to my grandmother, and my uncles became my guardians.

We had grown up in this atmosphere for a very long time. There was never a normal decade cycle without civil war. Everything only went backwards, and our lives became more than miserable. There was no employment, no schools, no hospitals. There was a marked spread of AIDS among the young people because of the high number of our sisters who survived on the streets. All the small businesses in the square were destroyed.

So we had to choose between rejoining the rebellion or dying under the cursed trees of the neighbourhood. After more than 50 years of independence, the country looked like a real human garbage bin. The capital has only one university, one stadium, a 13-storey building, and some lousy restaurants.

The frantic retreat of the Banyamoulengué was widespread. They fled to their country of origin, abandoning the loot behind them. In the city centre, a large fire was lit and was to be used as a large massacre furnace. Hundreds of Banyamoulengué were thrown into this large fire to the cheers of the spectators. In a small alley in Lakouanga, seven Banyamoulengué were arrested. The people pounced on them and started throwing large rocks at them. They died on the spot in a great stupefaction. Only the Banyamoulengué who left the country in time were saved. The rest succumbed to the lynch mobs

After a week of intense fighting, the Kota regime fell and passed under the reign of the new president, Boté, the rebel leader. Women and young girls marched naked in the city of Bangui to express their joy, celebrate the fall of the Kota regime, and proclaim the victory and arrival of the liberators. The Chadian mercenaries were also received as kings, saviours. Pieces of loincloths were spread out everywhere as these liberators passed by. The people, who had suffered everything, entrusted themselves completely to Boté and expected a new era in which everything had to change radically.

Chapter 11

Alas, we were born and raised in war in a country of madmen! For more than five decades, our country has been living in a steady rhythm of military–political unrest. How can one believe that the people would be an object of manipulation? Governing a people is not a matter of chance, and not everyone is called upon to lead a people. However, in Central Africa, everything seems to start from a game. People get up one fine morning and declare themselves politicians. People can get out of bed and go into the bush to rebel. And this is in whose name? The Central African people, of course! All these crimes are committed in the name of the people, despite the fact that they are the greatest victims.

There can be no greater leader than one who gives his whole life for his people. He can never be at peace if does not think about improving the living conditions of his people. He must think of everything, dare everything, do everything for them. In principle, his nights should be less peaceful if he does not work to respond to the expectations of the people.

But we have developed without an effective organization of our society, and nature has had the great misfortune to provide us with narrow-minded leaders, those without vision and without consistent policies. We are an unhappy people who have been sunk in abject misery. Worse, our state is not shaping us for the near future. The education and health systems are collapsing, sinking badly. Those leading us find nothing to do but to take away our parents, our older brothers who dare to say no to the system. All those who switch to the opposition must choose between exile or death.

A great machine of repression is marching over the life and liberty of the people. We are nailed down and mistreated. Nepotism, clanism, and regionalism become the hallmarks of luxury. Everyone is drowning in falsehood and corruption. Thus, we are witnessing an alienation from life. To survive, many people are forced to change birth certificates and identity cards, in order to obtain a birth certificate or a card whose details make them relatives of the ruling clan.

So, we have to change our name, our region, to hide our ethnic origin. Without this, no one other than those in power can have a job. The traffickers in false documents line their pockets, and their market has become lucrative. In this way, the administration is filled with incompetent officials, stuffed with fake diplomas.

You cannot think of governing a country with muscles. Man is the most sociable being there is.

Boté, who was acclaimed by the people, revels in totally rotten governance. He steals state property, signing secret contracts with transnationals to exploit mining resources and selling off some of these resources completely. He makes large amounts of money and sets up secret bank accounts in Switzerland and a number of tax havens. He gathers around him only his family, his in-laws, his friends and girlfriends, his concubines, his whole village.

The city is full of weird, crazy-looking people. The national administration begins to suffer turmoil. A flood of early retirements is decreed to renew the staff. Afterward, Boté rearranges the administration of the personnel. The orderlies become general managers and office employee managers. And what happens? Everyone has to get a slice of the cake, to think about building a beautiful villa, to own luxury cars? Send his children to saunter around in Europe?

But how long is this going to last? To repress the protests, Boté builds two torture camps, secret prisons. And the two most famous camps are Roux camp, located upstream of the presidential palace, and Bossembélé camp, located hundreds of kilometres from the capital.

None of those who enter these camps can come out alive. Death is a daily occurrence.

Chapter 12

Another rebel organization emerges in the north of the country. Its name is Seleka, which means 'coalition'. It is a coalition of all the rebel movements in the country. According to the leaders of the various groups, this alliance is formed at the price of the freedom of Central African people. With this, everything suggests that the people were cursed because of the unrest and successive civil wars that disrupted the course of events. Nothing works any more for the people, so freedom and development have been confiscated by the powerful. The people are starving to death because they cannot go fishing or to the fields, for fear of being beheaded by 'road cutters'. Banditry, delinquency, and vandalism have reached their apogee. The villages are emptying of their populations in a large rural exodus to Bangui, where everything is concentrated.

Thus, the sound of Seleka has found a particular resonance in the ears of the population, especially among the unemployed youth. The minds of the population are agitated, and young and old everywhere decide to join the ranks of Seleka. Everyone talks about 'freedom', 'justice', 'equality'. However, no one takes the time to reflect on these different terms.

There are practically no schools in the provincial towns to provide basic education to the villagers, nor hospitals for their care. These populations are dying from everything and nothing; malaria and acute diarrhoea have become deeply entrenched. However, others in others places can beat their breasts: 'We have the best schools in the world, the best hospitals in the world, the best police in the world ....'. But what remains to us and connects us with life is merely our breath. Nothing more than that. The future seems to be growing darker for us.

People are even afraid to go to the hospitals, where death is provided free of charge— on account of the incompetence and ineffectiveness of the medical staff, who are poorly trained in most cases. This is the cause of many tragic deaths. Some of these staff are even sent as regional health leaders. What a crime! As a result, Seleka was formed from the great abused mass of the socially forsaken, a great evil born of the mismanagement of state resources, where corruption, embezzlement of public funds, and nepotism rot the collective mentality.

The Seleka movement becomes important because people join it day and night. The government does not know what measures to adopt to stop the interest of young people in Seleka. Defections within the national defence forces no longer count. Boté was rejected by the entire population. There are people of all ethnicities, all beliefs, all religions, all races within Seleka. 'Long live freedom!' 'Long live justice!' These slogans are constantly repeated.

The advance of Seleka is slow but steady. The first villages and towns in the north fall into the hands of Seleka.

The Seleka movement entered the village of Yeti during a hot summer afternoon. As a result, the whole village panicked, given the widespread savage turmoil of Seleka in the area. Seleka were tasked with taking control of the entire village and surrounding all its exits. In consequence, the entry and exit routes were controlled, so no one could enter or leave. Sahamat, the chief rebel Seleka, seized upon a villager in order to get him to point out the residence of the chief of this invaded village. No sooner said than done. He was presented with a bamboo house consisting of four main rooms, around which were arranged the homes of the chief's four wives.

The Yeti chief was seized and dragged outside, and his four wives and their children too. The children began to cry, while the women trembled with fear. Sahamat demanded in an authoritative tone to be served food. Yeti ordered his first wife to oblige. She timidly entered the room she occupied, to take out a plate of chicken seasoned with tomato sauce, accompanied by brown rice. Sahamat despised this hospitable gesture, overturned the plate, and demanded that it be replaced immediately.

Yeti's wife returned to her husband to ask him for advice. He advised her to kill three chickens to roast and for a white sauce to use the good game that his trap had just caught. Listening to this proposal, the rebel leader demanded that two young goats also be killed for the members of his unit and for himself. Without any argument, his orders were carried out to the letter.

Yeti's wives prepared two delicious dishes for the general, while his men took charge themselves of preparing the young goats. Sahamat was served his grilled chickens and his white game sauce, which he ate with a large ball of cassava. He enjoyed himself; he was served the milk alcohol Ngouli, which he took happily. Similarly, his men went to fill up the cans of the sellers of milk alcohol, which they shared with each other to accompany their meal.

Sahamat called one of his men, who came to inject him with a drug to deaden his conscience. Immediately, this gesture was followed stupidly by the whole group, who also injected themselves with the drug. A strange sensation seized everyone, so that a hideous agitation pushed them to the extreme. First, Sahamat asked for Yeti's youngest wife, a very beautiful and sweet woman, as well as his two daughters, aged 14 to 16 years.

He was given one of Yeti's dwellings, that of his first wife. It was a large space containing three bedrooms, one of which is the main one where Yeti's young wife was tied to the bed. The daughters had their hands tied and were kept in the same room as their young mother.

Sahamat grabbed the woman. She resisted him with all her might. She said no to Sahamat and spat in his face. He became terribly irritated. He pulled out his knife and demanded again that she give up her body. But her refusal was categorical.

'I am for my master and my body is for him alone,' the young woman said. 'I cannot give myself to you.'

'You belong to your master, huh?' replied Sahamat. 'Do you want me to kill him, bitch?'

Immediately, Sahamat ordered that Yeti be brought to him. Once they had brought him, the guards, under Sahamat's order, brutally bound him. Without hesitation, Sahamat, before the eyes of the rebellious young woman, dragged her husband under a mango tree. All the other women and children began to cry.

Yeti's first wife ran to plead for her husband, begging Sahamat's forgiveness. She said she was willing to have sex with him if he deigned to release her husband. But as an answer, Sahamat slapped her hard in face and had her thrown to the ground. Sahamat seized Yeti again. He pulled out his knife and cut off his head with all his force.

Seeing this, the wife who had come to Yeti's aid went wild and fell on Sahamat, beating him with her fists. Sahamat turned with the knife and stabbed her. She fell dead next to her husband.

In the meanwhile, all the villagers took refuge in their respective huts. They watched the scene helplessly through the holes in the windows. Many of them were shaking in panic. Sahamat returned very agitated, grabbing again a young woman to rape her. But the woman was stronger than he was, so he could not do it alone. His men came to his assistance, preventing the woman's actions. They grabbed her hands and forcibly opened her intertwined feet to allow Sahamat to penetrate her. They spread her legs apart and immobilized her, allowing Sahamat to rape her without trouble. He raped that poor woman ruthlessly. And as she had irritated him too much, he shot her in the head once he had been satisfied. The two girls tied up in the same room fainted on the spot, unable to bear such cruelty. Sahamat mocked their bleak despondency and warned them not to resist him as their young mother had done.

Meanwhile, some of Sahamat's men went to the village huts, where they also seized the women and girls from the village to rape them. A great calamity had struck the village of Yeti. Tears and wailing were heard everywhere. And no one could fly to their aid. At night, only the stars gave of their light. And in the sky, a shower of bullets rang out and the sky turned red.

The village slept under the rattle of the guns. Husbands who dared to oppose the rape of their wives were killed. All this happened in the indifference of nature, silent and gloomy. In the distance, we heard the cry of jackals and the waves of the Tomi River. The grass rippled in a cockroach dance as a bitter wind passed by. The villagers who tried to escape were gunned down.

Afterward, on Sahamat's orders, able-bodied men from the village along with children were rounded up, willingly or forcibly, to be recruited into the ranks of Seleka.

The new recruits from the village had to undergo their baptism of fire. This was organized around a large fire, as in an initiates' camp. Then the rookies had to go naked in front of the clothed veterans, to be hazed. The first mission of this baptism was to inure the rookies to fear. So they were made to lie on the ground, and shots of all calibres rang out over their heads. The weaker ones cried, trembled, and shit themselves. The next morning, small sessions related to the initiation were repeated. The new recruits thus accepted a new imposed lifestyle. They had to learn to kill, to accustom themselves to blood—and, therefore, to kill easily. Seleka sought by all means to remove all that was human from the recruits in order to steep them in cruelty, in monstrousness. The men of the village were gathered in large numbers and enrolled in the coalition. They were told that this would help them to have another life, better than the miserable life in which they had groaned ...

Seleka decided to leave the village early in the morning, to march to the capital. For this purpose, they had to take provisions with them—so they plundered the village, emptying the village's granaries and taking away a large number of cattle. They also took some women and children into captivity as sex slaves. From time to time, they started up this ritual song:

'We are the warriors of blood.

Suffering is a friend, death a vulgar bogeyman.

Courage and determination will lead us to glory.

Happiness awaits us at the end of the road.'

The march was slow. Seleka had to have the approval and then the support of the entire population. They intended to increase the rapprochement with the people they met along the march and explain to them the validity of the movement. The population supported them in large numbers, because of the misery everyone had lived through.

Chapter 13

A very large division began to be felt in the ranks of Seleka. Among the Central Africans involved in this coalition, there were also Chadian and Sudanese mercenaries. As a result, a Seleka fringe of Muslim allegiance was formed against the rest of the Christian-majority group. Cohesion within the group was gradually eroded, leading to mistrust of each other. The Muslim fringe, made up of brave and seasoned warriors, took control of Seleka and led the march toward the capital, Bangui. No one was to dispute orders, and what was decided was carried out promptly.

It was reported that on the march of Seleka toward the capital, the violence, killings, and looting were directed against a single community: the Christian community. Thus, in the provincial cities that fell under Seleka control, churches began to be looted. Many of the nuns of Catholic convents were raped and priests were murdered. Entire churches were burned. Missionary vehicles were stolen, and huge reserves of fuel and large sums of money were carried off.

The Christian fringe began to denounce the abuses committed against its community. But, unfortunately, nothing could stop this tendency; on the contrary, it intensified. The Muslim fringe began to silently eliminate Christian militiamen among its ranks, to gain dominance over the group. Then, the Christian militiamen broke away, moving in a different direction, abandoning the group. This division destroyed the principal vision of Seleka, which had been only to free the people from misery and all political evils.

The coalition arrived in the town of Bouka. A team was immediately set up to monitor the location. Sahamat set up a strategic plan for the attack on the city. Strategic points, such as the military camp, the gendarmerie, and the prefecture building, were studied. They attacked these places at night—without any real resistance, because the population had abandoned the regime. They seized abandoned military vehicles and looted the local public treasury. They did not find the prefect, who—abandoning the population—had taken care to leave the city for Bangui when the advance of Seleka was announced on community radio.

Afterward, the group decided to attack the local bishopric. They entered the great enclosure of St. Theresa's Cathedral and broke into the chancellery, where the bishop's residence is. A few minutes later, a large body was dragged out, obviously that of the bishop, wearing his clerical cassock. Sahamat threatened him with death, demanding the group be given 30 million CFA francs.

'I have nothing on me; I'm only a servant of God,' the bishop moaned. 'Where would I get such a large amount of money from?'

Sahamat spat on him.

'Are you just a servant of God? And don't the servants of God eat, huh? Isn't it you who are ripping off people with your tale of offerings and tithes? I'm not obliged to ask you twice. I advise you not to push me to the limit or waste my time.'

At the same instant, Sahamat demanded that the bishop be tied up hand and foot by the *arbatacha* method, where one is brutally bound with both upper and lower limbs fixed behind one's back. A rag was shoved into his mouth. Then Sahamat ordered that the bishop's fingers be cut off. Sahamat's huge, sturdy bodyguard, Mola, pulled out his knife and stretched out the hand of the bishop, who was already shaking dreadfully. Mola, without a moment's reflection, cut off the bishop's index finger, from which an enormous amount of blood spurted. While the bishop struggled, Mola then cut off his thumb. Large tears streamed from the bishop's eyes, and his clothes were soaked in blood.

At the same time, Sahamat's men undertook a full search of the bishopric, in particular of the chancellery—from where they took Mass wines, fuel, and missionary vehicles. In addition, a large safe was discovered in the bishop's room. After trying unsuccessfully to open it, they took it to Sahamat. He told them that the only person able to open the safe was the bishop. Sahamat removed the rag from the bishop's mouth and advised him to give him the password to the safe. The latter refused and stubbornly resisted.

As a result, Sahamat asked his men to pass him a pair of pliers. He began to pull out, one by one, the teeth of the bishop, who was held immobile by three strong men. The bishop's face swelled up immediately and he was completely drenched in blood. He groaned in pain and asked for death. He could no longer resist the torture, never having been accustomed to it.

Sahamat changed tactics, planning to gouge out the bishop's eye. As he moved forward to perform his new tactic, the bishop gave the password in an agonized and scarcely audible voice. Opening the safe, Sahamat discovered about 50 million in the safe, along with gold and diamonds. He cried out and performed a shrill, rogue dance to express his joy. He took away all the treasure, leaving the bishop at the mercy of his men. As he took a few steps toward the exit, he heard a gunshot. The bishop had just been killed by Mola, receiving a bullet in the head. His secretary and four other priests were also killed.

A hundred metres from the chancellery was the convent of the Poor Clare Sisters. Seleka decided to go there. They broke in at the moment when the nuns had taken refuge in their chapel, 'Mary, Mother of Pilgrims'. The nuns were all terrified, because they had followed from a distance what had happened at the bishopric. Sahamat and his powerful bodyguard, Mola, entered the sacristy, looking for the mother superior or the bursar. They found no one there. So they went out and asked the group of nuns who had taken refuge in the chapel:

'Who's in charge of this place?'

A deathly silence hung over the room. The nuns were shaking with fear. Some of them started to wet themselves, while others sobbed. Sahamat took the safety catch off his gun, engaged a bullet, and fired a shot into the air. The sisters well and truly panicked and instinctively broke into singing the *Ave Maria*. Sahamat saw that his approach had not been the correct one. He went to grab one of the nuns and pointed a gun at her head, whispering in her ear:

'Tell me who's in charge of you and I won't make you suffer; your life will be spared.'

She was shaking severely and was of little use to him. Annoyed, Sahamat shot her in the head. The nun collapsed and died immediately. Sahamat went on hysterically to grab another nun and cut off her head in fury. Seeing these horrors, the whole chapel was shaking with panic and sobbing. But all the exits were guarded well, so no one could escape. The bursar nun stood up and surrendered to ease the situation. Sahamat gave her a pair of strong slaps in the face for having wasted his time.

'Are you the one in charge?' Sahamat demanded.

'Yes, I am,' replied the sister.

'Then give me everything you have as funds here: money, gold, diamonds—everything,' Sahamat began.

'We don't have everything you're asking for.'

She led him in the direction of the convent, where the bursar's office was.

While Sahamat, Mola, and the bursar went to the office, the other militias fell upon the sisters huddled in the chapel. Everyone grabbed a nun, and the commotion began. There were dramatic tussling movements, rough grapplings in scenes of pitiful violence. A nun who resisted being raped was bound to the large crucifix in the chapel and petrol was poured over her. She was burned because of her resistance and failure to obey. Another nun, very young and beautiful, who was soaked in tears and consumed with fear, irritated an old man who had enlisted in Seleka. He called for help from two other militiamen, who seized the nun and tied her up in order to prevent her from struggling again. The old man was so irritated that he no longer wanted this young nun; he dragged her to the ground after virulent insults, drew his knife, and stabbed her. He ripped open her abdomen and pulled out her entrails and her heart. Even that was not enough; he cut off her breasts and urinated on her.

The nuns went to sleep in shame and devastation. They had just been outraged and humiliated. Their dignity had been trampled upon, as well as their sacred femininity. They lost all their identity.

From the bursar's office, Sahamat listened to the sound of weapons and the actions of his men. He therefore urged the bursar to hurry. She opened a small briefcase hidden in a cupboard, containing about 10 million CFA francs. This sum was reserved for the running of the convent for at least one trimester. Sahamat took the sum of money and gathered up the Mass wines and the hosts, which he cheerfully bit into. He decided that his unit could billet itself there in the convent for a while.

The militiamen scraped the bottoms of the pots to find something to eat. They went to get rice, oil, and other supplies from the bursar's to cook a meal. They prepared a sauce with a young goat they had killed in the convent's herd. It was a great celebration. They ate, drank, and screwed like dogs set free. Sahamat chose the bursar's room, where he spent the night with a 15-year-old girl, one of the deceased Yeti's children. She was his sex slave. He screwed her all night, drunk on alcohol and drugs.

The following morning, Sahamat gathered his men together to leave the city. But the latter continued to sleep after their wild evening. As they left the locality, they took seven vehicles with them, five from the chancellery and two from the nun's convent. Also, a large reserve of fuel, bags of rice, and cans of oil were taken away.

They left the city for a small village 75 km away, but they took more than 14 hours to get there because of the poor state of the roads. When they arrived, the whole population was frozen with fear because they had heard about the massacres and hideous acts perpetrated by this gang of killers. The militiamen inspected the buildings, but the village did not seem to be a favourable location; there was nothing special about it. Seleka attacked a small Protestant church where the panicked population had taken refuge. They surrounded the place, sealing off the exits. Sahamat ordered the church to be set on fire.

From inside the church, those who had taken refuge observed the scene in great agitation. They saw how the rebels brought cans of petrol and approached to pour it on the building. Already, however, the 'save whoever can' impulse implicit in such dreadful events took hold of the population, and a mob stormed the rebels and overwhelmed them. The rebels who had been placed in the rear saved the situation. They opened fire on the crowd, who fell dead under the hail of bullets. Some people escaped the massacre and fled into the woods.

Everyone made way for Sahamat, who walked with his head held high among the corpses, mocking them and spitting on them. He regarded himself as being above the gods: immortal, untouchable. His men took a short break to allow Sahamat to rest and eat before continuing on the road. He leaned against a large mango tree on a wooden stool prepared for this occasion, displaying his loot: gold, diamonds, and a large sum of money. He gleefully contemplated his treasure and foresaw a bright future for himself, a beautiful life in the sun—for he had lived so long in the shadow.

Sahamat looked at his men and asked himself the question: 'Should I give them a share of the money?' He resigned himself to squandering his fortune. But he had earned it with the others. He called Mola to ask him for advice. Mola looked him straight in the eye, saying to him:

'To be in good terms with them, you have to look after them.'

'But we must buy weapons,' replied Sahamat.

'Yes, but if you don't take care of them, they'll start to misbehave and won't obey you anymore,' Mola said.

'No longer obey me? Whoever disobeys me will deserve death. And I'm absolutely uncompromising.'

'Do you think you can march on Bangui alone? It's with these men that you'll succeed,' Mola said.

'I'll replace them with other men,' shouted Sahamat, annoyed.

'Whom you'll then kill on a whim.'

'No, goddammit! Stop contradicting me.' Sahamat took small steps, turning around where he was, haunted by greed.

'And what do you advise me to do?' he asked.

'You have to give them something symbolic,' Mola replied.

'I buy them guns and drugs and feed them—and you want me to give them ... Anything but that! They have everything they need to get by. And from now on, I'm not going to feed them. Gather them all together and I'll talk to them.'

Mola had them sit down so that Sahamat could transmit his message. Sahamat raised his head, walking into the middle of his grouped men. He hesitated to give his message; but in a reckless gesture, he hammered out these words:

'People of Central Africa! Duty calls us. It tells us to say no to the tyranny, marginalization, and misery that blights us. We have been excessively marginalized, and this society has turned its back on us—a great injustice born of the under-representation of our community in the management of public affairs. Our goods and merchandise are constantly being misappropriated by the police. We are being called strangers, the sons of whores. So, do we have to stay like this so that these guys can fuck us in the ass? No, we have to act to put an end to this. And it's with you that we'll do it. We'll build a new, more just, equitable, prosperous, and peaceful society. And I'm asked what I'm going to give you to win this gamble?

'I have nothing to give you or guarantee you. You are the masters of your destiny, and it's a new story being written in which you're the main actors. It's my duty to train you and show you the right thing to do. Therefore, I can give you what's necessary for your survival. I give you the weapons with which you're going to defend yourselves. These weapons are your father and your mother. Never think that I'll give you more than that, because you have what's necessary in your own hands. These weapons are extremely expensive, and I can't afford to buy them for you and at the same time give you money—because when the ammunition runs out, it will have to be replaced. You'll manage to feed yourselves from now on. But don't create a mess, because our struggle is not limited to what you eat or to getting you money. It goes far beyond that. You have to have a good job to change your standard of living, once we win victory and this regime is overthrown. After that, you'll all be rewarded; but woe to those who die, because their hope will be limited to the grave. To hell with their corpses!'

A great silence took hold of everyone, and each one withdrew on his side. Sahamat was not a man to argue with about things; either his orders were implemented or he killed you. Only Mola, his close bodyguard, held his head up a little.

Chapter 14

Muslims are a minority but hold a monopoly on trade in the country. They are large livestock breeders and lead important businesses in the services sector. They are therefore among the wealthiest section of the population and have gradually settled throughout the country. However, the organization of political and social life is such that the ordinary people live in unparalleled poverty. Police officers and soldiers get between 54,000 and 60,000 CFA francs as monthly pay. And this has changed, because the salary used to be lower than this. As a result, the police and soldiers are completely caught up in corruption, which is the greatest evil in Central Africa. They extort money from merchants and travellers. So, the merchants, who are generally Muslims, have been subjected to a lot of police abuses. To properly characterize the police, a label was applied to them: they are aliens—they come to enrich themselves at our expense.

One day, we were returning from a holiday and we were on our way back to the small seminary in Sibut. When we arrived at a police station more than 75 km from Bangui, we saw a large number of people arrested at a checkpoint, all of them Muslims. They all had their national identity cards or the documents required for their free movement throughout the country. But the police demanded 50,000 CFA francs from each one before letting them pass through the checkpoint barrier. And meanwhile, another group, whose leader had approached the chief of the control service, complained about their fate—because they had spent two days without food at the checkpoint, and they were condemned to weeding and cleaning the premises, as they had no money to pay for their release. They were working under the direct sun, and this did not bother the police officers at all, who were still waiting for their bribes.

In addition, the police created all kinds of more or less serious offences to charge them with in order to squeeze more money out of them. Like this other case, a Muslim passenger was arrested at the Dekoa checkpoint. He was on public transport, and he was made to get off and asked to show his identity papers. While he was in a panic to present his papers, another policeman discreetly slipped a packet of hemp into his bag. They then accused him of trafficking in hemp, sent him immediately to solitary confinement at the post, and demanded a heavy fine of 750,000 for his release.

Similarly, police and soldiers used to steal the herds from Fulani or Muslim herders, who regularly moved around in search of good pasture. It is enough to accuse them of being 'road blockers' to be able to rob them. Thus, a difficult life was imposed on them, and the plight of this community was seldom listened to.

Furthermore, the Central African Republic suffers from major security problems. Since the police, gendarmes, and military are all corrupt, a marked porosity of the borders jeopardizes territorial integrity. They sell the country for the benefit of their bellies. As a result, Sudanese and Chadian poachers and mercenaries exploit the border porosity to destabilize the country.

Many weapons of war easily cross our borders and our checkpoints, in exchange for meagre sums of money. It is enough to introduce the weapons into bags of cassava, groundnuts, cotton, or coal, preparing for each checkpoint a small sum of 5,000 francs to dissuade the police from imposing meticulous inspections. Weapons were therefore sold like bread at our borders, under the complicit gaze of our security forces. This negligence and corruption has benefited the massive penetration of foreign mercenaries.

Meanwhile, everything was centralized in Bangui, and the provinces were completely abandoned. There was zero organizational or functional autonomy at the level of the local communities. Decentralization presupposes issuing a directive for all decisions in a vertical and irreversible way. But no initiative was proposed for effective decentralization with regard to the exploitation or free management of regional economic assets.

There could be two or three qualified doctors for a region with a population of thousands. Health centres were almost non-existent or not at all properly equipped. Over a distance of more than 150 km, there may not be any health centre, let alone health workers. In addition, schools were badly built. Some children had to travel 50 km a day to get to school, with nothing to eat. The children drank cassava on a daily basis without any possible variation in diet, thus damaging their health.

Chapter 15

After Sahamat's talk, everyone understood that from now on his life was in his own hands and that only his weapon could satisfy his needs. Crimes and violence against the population increased, stripping them of their property. Sahamat, once he had rested, prepared to move the camp. They had to leave this city for a large mining city, called the City of Light. But before that, a team of Sudanese and Chadian mercenaries had to arrive, to strengthen the coalition, before reaching the City of Light. These mercenaries were to arrive with new weapons of war. These weapons came largely from Libya—now weakened by terrorism—through Darfur.

The new Seleka team was formed with the arrival of new, self-proclaimed mercenary generals, 65% of whom were Muslims. Dotasun and Abtasun imposed themselves and demanded that they also should be raised up to head the coalition.

To do this, Mola, Sahamat's fearsome bodyguard, had to be removed. In the Central African Republic, Muslims were discredited; they were rough people who could not be integrated into the general administration or fully supervised. This community has suffered for more than half a century and was really marginalized. They were less represented in the state and outraged on the grounds of the overrunning of the Central African Republic. They came from elsewhere. They were not Central Africans. Now, they all came out of nowhere, except for the pygmies.

The reconstitution of Seleka changed the face of this group. A new posture, a new vision was forged: to reduce inequalities, to remove marginalization against the Muslim community. Also, the rise of extremism and radicalization around the world reinforced this vision. Thus, the arrival of Sudanese and Chadians in the coalition encouraged the idea of revenge and the forced spread of Islam. In the coalition, more than 65% of the population were ruled by Islam, as against about 20% Christian and the rest animist. The march to Bangui became difficult because of the ethnic and religious considerations that penetrated the group. There was hatred in the hearts of Muslims; they sought revenge by any means possible and a way of dispelling hesitation and overcoming prejudices and suspicions about Islam, a religion which others had long demonized. However, great intellectual, social, and political poverty also contributed to community divisions. There was a lack of effective and fundamental secularism and a consequent lack of democracy, which could otherwise lead to religious tolerance.

The Seleka coalition left the small village at night for the City of Light. Already, one felt the division, and certain affinities developed. Christians became attached to Mola and Muslims to Sahamat and Dotasun. A first operation targeted a large Protestant church. At this, Mola stepped forward and objected: no church could be touched again. But this opposition changed the order of things. Sahamat and

Dotasun found Mola's intervention too much. They came toward him and hurled these words at him:

'Who do you think you are to block our way?'

'I'm one of the leaders of this group, and I won't allow anyone to undermine the vision we have: freeing the Central African people from the yoke of poverty and rebuilding our society into a better, just, and egalitarian society ....'

'Just and egalitarian? Don't you know that we Muslims are the lower class in this nation? What injustice have we not suffered?' shouted Sahamat. 'The police and gendarmes fuck us in the ass all day long and endlessly strip us left and right of our herds. And you call that justice?'

'That's what we're fighting about, Sahamat,' Mola replied. 'It's time to change things, to think about a new era, to heal hearts.'

'It's not your business; we'll take care of it.'

At this point, a Chadian mercenary who understood neither Sango nor French interfered in the debate and questioned Sahamat in Arabic. They exchanged a few words in Arabic, after which the mercenary radically changed expression. Other mercenaries gathered and surrounded Mola—who, a moment ago, had been Sahamat's right-hand man. They demanded that he drop his weapon. Mola refused categorically and prepared himself for the worst. Given the rising tension, he slipped the safety catch off his weapon.

Mola dodged a shot from a Kalashnikov and retaliated with all his Christian men. A heavy gunfight broke out between the two sides. Mola led his team and resisted until his last breath. A Sudanese mercenary shot him from a distance in the head. He fell on the spot. The Muslims managed to overcome Mola and the rest of his group, as the Christians were in the minority. However, considerable loss of life was sustained on both sides.

Sahamat refused to inflict harm on the rest of the group and demanded that they not disobey him. He knew he could not exclude them. He chose to tone down his words and forbade harming the Christian fringe, in order to prevail in the conquest of power. The coalition marched seriously under Sahamat's guidance. On the way, a large part of the Muslim population joined the movement on a massive scale.

This military advance spread delight throughout the Muslim community, and the group grew larger. Small subgroups with different leaders were formed. They all took the name of Seleka. At a certain point, the members of one subgroup could no longer obey another. This situation became widespread and created confusion.

Several Muslim traders took advantage of this disorder and embarked on looting, robberies, and violence. These Muslims were haunted by the spirit of revenge that was spreading in the coalition. However, no one was supporting the established regime. All the state soldiers threw away their weapons because of the extreme poverty that was rife and the bad governance and nepotism that characterized the regime. So this situation led to a general revolt, and no one was opposed to the advance of Seleka. The fact that several subgroups joined Seleka posed the problem of determining a hierarchy. The militias acted on their own initiative. The widespread lootings were accompanied by the destruction of private property.

The City of Light is a large, strategic city, also abounding in considerable economic assets. About ten gold and diamond mines aroused the greed of miners and rebel groups. Thus, Seleka's first objective was to conquer all the mining sites and to impose its supremacy. This was achieved after three days of intense fighting between Seleka and a group of well-armed, illegally installed miners.

Seleka established itself and introduced heavy, illegal taxes. The lootings, killings, and massacres drove people to take refuge in the bush. Targeted attacks, on the basis of ethnic and religious affiliation, increased. Men, women, and children were kidnapped; public buildings were destroyed.

Moreover, the population that fled into the bush had nothing to eat. They ate yams and wild leaves; they drank unsafe water that caused acute diarrhoea and other more serious diseases in children and the elderly.

Since Seleka were not interested in remaining in the City of Light, Sahamat decided to create a rear base in this city to continue the exploitation and sale of products, and the money gained thereby was used to buy weapons.

Seleka left the City of Light and were now 380 km from Bangui. The threat became more significant, and the Bangui regime became more and more agitated. President Boté was crying out for help from the international community to stop the advance of Seleka. In the meantime, several peace and post-crisis agreements had been signed—which he then trampled underfoot. He launched a government of national unity with Seleka to save the situation, but it came to nothing.

Chapter 16

Boté was deposed and power spilled out onto the streets. Seleka attacked the main prison, where political opponents and some rebel activists were illegally detained. All the weapons depots were destroyed and weapons proliferated. The AK-47s sold for 1,000 francs and grenades for 25 francs. Everyone, even the children, had two or more weapons. The law of the jungle was established, and widespread looting and mass killings became part of the daily life of the Banguissois.

The self-proclaimed President Dotasun could not control his men. Meanwhile, the number of militias was increasing dramatically. Dotasun tried to restrict the lists of their members in order to avoid the worst. He therefore rejected en masse all the men that joined the coalition. The international community turned its back on him and failed to recognize his power. Thus, he could not pay the mercenaries that had arrived and he sent them home. He advised Chadian and Sudanese mercenaries to pay themselves, at the expense of the population and businesses. And with a willing religious solidarity, the grand coalition of Muslim-majority Seleka flung itself on non-Muslim communities.

Chadian and Sudanese mercenaries went from house to house looting. Everyone had to enrich himself before returning to his country of origin. Large firms like Total and CFAO were looted. In addition, hundreds of Toyota and Renault vehicles were transported to Chad and Sudan.

Targeted killings and sexual violence against the non-Muslim population grew worse. These actions outraged the population and encouraged the birth of armed resistance. The population, including the FACA (Central African Armed Forces), used violent methods to stop Seleka. The resistance was described as pro-Boté, and President Dotasun decided to savagely repress this resistance.

Non-Muslim neighbourhoods were targeted by the ruling government. Seleka entered them and proceeded door-to-door to track down the pro-Boté elements. They shot anything that moved. Men, women, and children—all without exception were targeted. Terror invaded the city, and many people fled the massacres and took refuge in Congo and Cameroon.

In the KM5 neighbourhoods, which are predominantly Muslim, the abuses were even more horrific. All non-Muslim servants were rounded up and taken to torture chambers. They were beheaded, disembowelled, and thrown into wells. And around the houses, the ground was littered with corpses covered with large swarms of flies.

A month after Seleka's seizure of power on 23 March 2013, our lives began to be threatened. The Seleka militias had gone out of control and were acting brutally against the population. They were constantly attacking civilians and excelled in robberies and looting. The population were potential targets for repression due to the non-compliance with commitments to reward or allow the repatriation of particular mercenaries.

However, a part of the population believed that the arrival of Seleka would pave the way to a new era and wipe away the blunders and oppression of the ousted regime. But cases of violence, looting, and destruction of houses had begun to be recorded during the advance of Seleka into the provincial towns. Women and young girls were constantly being raped.

No one could approve of or be indifferent to the crimes committed. The Seleka militias were clearly beginning to attach themselves to one community to the detriment of others, directing the abuses and crimes against the areas of the Christian community. As a result, social cohesion, the harmony between the two communities, broke down. Both communities were bathed in blood.

On Friday, 12 April 2013, a young man was run over by a patrol vehicle of Seleka, marked 'Le Risqueur de Bouroumata', in the 7th *arrondissement*— specifically in the Ngatoua district, a few metres from the Kassaï camp. This outraged the inhabitants, who took to the streets to express their indignation. As a result, the ruling regime gave a reason to repress the demonstration, saying that the people were pro-Boté types and wanted to harm the ruling party.

Thus, a significant force of Seleka militiamen was deployed in the *arrondissement*, with a mission to eliminate all pro-Boté elements. There was nothing to do; this force was just to march on everything that moved. At about 4:00 p.m., our *arrondissement* was invaded and heavy weapons' gunfire began to ring out everywhere. There was widespread panic and no one could wait a second to flee.

Some of the inhabitants huddled in their homes, as we fled and went to hide in Gbazoubangui hill. We were followed, and Seleka militiamen pursued us to where we were entrenched. They started to fire mortar shells and rockets at us. It was every man for himself! They spread out over the hill to hunt us down.

There was only one way out for us, the one leading to the Boy-rab district, near Ndress. The other routes were sealed off. The incoming fire had not failed to inflict casualties in our ranks. A friend of mine, Francus, had been shot in the head in the act of running away. He dropped dead on the spot. Another also, Audran, had both his legs blown off by shell fire that allowed no survival; he died after a brief movement. Yet another, Slach, had fallen on the sharp branch of a tree, which had pierced his entrails. My heart was pounding as though it would burst, and I could not stop to help the others. In my flight, I had been hit in the face and grazed by my passage through the tree branches. I was slightly injured.

We finally arrived in the Boy-rab district, where the inhabitants started to harass us with questions. Some of us answered these questions. But I could not speak at all, because I was shaking continuously. I immediately decided to leave the neighbourhood, taking a taxi. I went to Sica1 to a close relative's house, as I had no one to welcome me in Boy-rab.

When I arrived in Sical, I passed the night there as mute as I had been in Boy-rab. My relatives could understand my shock. I was jumping with fright at the slightest sound. Everything frightened me, and I stayed glued to my relatives. It was without doubt the beginning of a psychological disorder.

The following morning, I received a call from a brother, Olden, who was returning from the Orobé refugee camp, a village somewhat distant from the town of Zongo, on the other side of the Oubangui River in Democratic Congo. A mass of Central Africans found refuge there. Olden came back to get his things and he advised me to follow him to the refuge, to shelter me too from the violence and mass killings. I could not think before giving my answer, which was certainly positive because I was beginning to be seriously revolted by the actions of Seleka.

In the meantime, we were informed that the attack by Seleka militia on the Gbazoubangui hill had left more than 13 people dead, including six people who were praying in a small church situated at the bottom of the hill. Also, the militiamen proceeded to go door-to-door to hunt for Boté supporters. This had led to a lot of abuses, because most of the able-bodied men in the locality who had stayed at home were simply assaulted.

I crossed the same day Olden was supposed to return to the refugee camp. I went in to UNHCR management to register as a refugee. That day, I spent the night in the UNHCR shed. The next morning, a UNHCR convoy took us to Orobé, to the refugee camp, where I experienced another life.

Interlude II : The cry of hope

(written with Ephraim Tote)

Crack crack crack crack boom
Crack crack crack crack boom
A weapon, a sound, a man, a death.
Crack crack crack crack boom
Crack crack crack crack boom
Suffering, violence, movements,
Refugees.
Crack crack crack crack boom
Crack crack crack crack boom
My name is war, I'm meant to destroy,
rape, massacre.
I leave nothing in my path
Men, women, children
 I slaughter them
Ah ah ah ah ah ah ah
But who has deceived you?
My sufferings are as sweet as honey
Behold, I create rebellions, I invade cities
And humanity is waiting to be delivered
Ah ah ah ah ah ah ah
Look! I have my own who follow my will
Vandalism, I destroy state property
Communities, works of art
Tribalism, I divide men, peoples
Politics, the mother of hatred, squabbles
Battles, the lord of the dictatorship
The greatest African evil
My name is war

The blood that flows means absolutely nothing to
me
The loss of human lives is the driving force
The weapons I create
I give birth to orphans, widows
Internally displaced, refugees
The world is suffering from my pains
Ah ah ah ah ah ha ah
And you, my poor rival peace
What will you do for these men?
Crack crack crack crack boom
Crack crack crack crack boom
A weapon, a sound, a man, a death.
Crack crack crack crack boom
Crack crack crack crack boom
Suffering, violence, movements,
Refugees.
Oh I am peace! The greatest friend
Of humanity
I come to gather, to heal the pain
Unite the divided
In my heart I carry joy
Love, fraternity, solidarity
Forgiveness. It's the duty of a good father
Who loves all his children
Nothing causes more suffering than war
It's something I hate, something I detest
That I fight against
I'm not vandal, not tribal, not political.
I build, I unite, I democratize
No pain is felt in me

I dream of a better world
Look at all the things you're fighting war for
Men who have left their country
Separated from their parents
Sent to the grave, disappeared
Arrived in a foreign land,
All withdrawn, seeking shelter
Men of sorrows, suffering
The melancholy of the lost
Haunted by the uncertain future
Of an unfamiliar life
War is shabby and evil
Every day that passes
Every night that arrives
Immerses us in reflections
In spiritual battles
We are refugees
Let us become global citizens
We are here to open your doors
Because death has been watching out for us
We are looking for a protective shelter
A new life, more gentle and friendly
Oh we are refugees without cities
We cry out to you for our survival
The realization of our dream,
Our reintegration into the city
Nothing is greater than life
She is so beautiful if you feel protected
More tender if there is hope

Crack crack crack crack boom

Crack crack crack crack boom
A weapon, a sound, a man, a death.
Crack crack crack crack boom
Crack crack crack crack boom
Suffering, violence, movements,
Refugees.
Crack crack crack crack boom
Crack crack crack crack boom
You think you're flattering me with peace.
Eh eh eh eh eh eh eh eh eh eh
I'm not a monster.
They are men who shape me.
To fight against me, eliminate
Egoism, the thirst for power
The madness of grandeur, injustice ...
And there will be no more war, no more sorrow
No more separation, no more refugees.

Chapter 17

In Bangui, the non-Muslim community, supported by a new force called Antibalaka, organized itself to launch reprisals against the Muslim community.

On 5 December 2013, an outbreak of violence consumed the entire country. The Antibalaka were an unparalleled and murderous eruption. These people came up out of the abyss. They were equipped with protective *gris-gris*,[9] born of alliances with the powers of darkness. People said they seemed like they had gone to visit the devil himself. They had all kinds of knives, pieces of wood, arrows, and especially machetes bought in large numbers by the Boté regime for the extermination of opponents—in particular, of Seleka.

Thanks to these *gris-gris*, they could make astral journeys. They appeared and disappeared here and there, fighting invisible battles. The pacts signed with the powers of darkness forbade them from touching women and from eating certain foods, in order to avoid breaking their magical powers.

---

[9] Amulets worn for protection. *Gri-gris* are often associated with a tradition in Islam whereby a prayer written on paper is folded and then placed in a small leather pouch worn around the neck. In the context of CAR, however, it is the Antibalaka who are often associated with *gri-gris*. In this case, they do not contain Quranic verses and are often made of rolled-up plastic instead of leather. These *gri-gris* are associated with sorcery and are worn to make the wearer bullet-proof.

On 5 December, the Antibalaka attacked the strategic positions of Seleka. But they came up against a fortress, because Seleka were still well armed and in a position of strength. Seleka retaliated against the deadly incursion of the Antibalaka and inflicted bloody reprisals, which in a single day led to the deaths of more than 6,000 people.

The Antibalaka, supported by the FACA, decided to put an end to Seleka. They therefore strengthened their position and managed to tip the balance of power, thanks to the support of certain political leaders. The ball was now in the Antibalaka camp.

In all neighbourhoods, Seleka and Muslims became targets. A hunt for Muslims was organized everywhere. Machetes were distributed to everyone—men, women, and children—with a view to vengeance and the extermination of the Muslim community.

During those days, Muslims were pursued like animals. The weakest were caught up in their flight by hundreds of machete blows from all sides. We heard screams of torment, agonies from 'necklacing' with burning tyres,[10] savage machete blows: *tcha*, *tcha*, *tcha*, *tcha*, *tcha*. Muslims were decapitated in mid-flight, their heads springing into the air and falling onto the blood-drenched streets. Terror struck this community, delivered up to an unparalleled carnage.

---

[10] Necklacing: torture and extra-judicial execution by forcing a rubber tyre filled with petrol over a victim's head and arms and setting it alight.

A general jubilation revived the non-Muslim population, who had been living in the bush while fleeing the mass killings by Seleka. Even the people who were in exile in Congo returned to join the Antibalaka and took their revenge. Mosques and entire houses were destroyed, looted, and burned to the ground. There was no stone left on stone in Muslim neighbourhoods; all Muslim property was destroyed. Everything was stripped bare: mosques, schools, Association Musulmane en Afrique (AMA) centres. The Antibalaka reprisals exceeded all bounds. They also went door-to-door to eradicate Muslims.

In the ranks of the Antibalaka, a young man known as 'Chien Méchant'—whose whole family had been massacred by Seleka and who was the only survivor—excelled in violence against Muslims to revenge himself. He entered a Muslim home where the family was entrenched in a small room. With the help of his clan, he grabbed the father of the family. Chien Méchant decided to take care of this family on his own. He laid the old man on the ground and, eyes reddening with blood, started to decapitate him. He cut him into small pieces and ripped out his heart, which continued beating. From his pocket, he took out a *chikwangue*,[11] took a piece of the old man's flesh, and ate it. He ate the raw flesh and mocked the corpse. He cried out in vengeance for his murdered relatives. His friends followed his example, tore the

[11] Manioc bread in leaf wrapping, boiled and eaten as an accompaniment to vegetable and meat dishes.

108

old man to pieces, and also feasted on his flesh. Everyone cut off the part that seemed to him sweet and tossed it into his mouth as if in a horror film.

The old Muslim's wife and children were seized and dragged outside. Chien Méchant and his friends abandoned them to an agitated and raging mob. The mob immediately took over and beat the family to a pulp with heavy blows from pieces of wood, hammers, machetes. No holds barred. They succumbed, as the crowd grew larger and larger. Their bodies were thrown onto the street and burned with tyres.

In some marketplaces in the city of Bangui, human bodies were displayed, sold by butchers. They were murdered Muslims, burned and carefully cut up into pieces. Their skulls were exposed at the bottom of the sales tables. The butchers took pleasure in presenting them to passers-by as if in a sales auction. The Central African Republic had reached the depths of cruelty. It was profoundly bestialized. Human life lost its dignity and value. One could kill a human being like one would kill a chicken or a dog, without any qualms of conscience. The sanctity of life was dedicated to diabolical monstrousness ....

The Muslim community began to flee en masse from the massacres to neighbouring countries, to shelter from this barbarism.

The Antibalaka hung decapitated human heads and frightened people by their diabolical appearance. They entered the provincial cities on the hunt for Muslims. In addition, they targeted the Fulani community, from whom they carried away their herds and large sums of money. All transhumance routes were cut by the Antibalaka. They forgot the agreements they had signed and began to excel in the rape of women and children and in widespread looting.

After the Muslims had left the country en masse, the Antibalaka turned their barbarity against the people they had just liberated. They no longer made any distinction between Muslims and Christians. What mattered to them was to enrich themselves in one way or another. They wallowed in human blood, defying all the established authorities.

Chapter 18

When I arrived in Congo, I heaved a great sigh of relief, because I was far from the sound of guns, the tears, the bloodshed. I gradually came back to myself. I began to think about why we were in this crisis. In the end, I concluded that it was no less than stupidity.

My first nights in Congo were nightmarish and difficult. I continuously reviewed the acts of crime committed, those from which my friends had died. And, to be honest, the night-time frightened me very much. Around me, there was the sound of the other refugees, who also carried with them the heavy pain and suffering of the stupid crisis. The stories of others could be more terrible than mine, those whose close relatives were massacred in front of their eyes.

It was difficult for us to turn the page on this story in order to think about the future. The refugee camp at Orobé had a forlorn atmosphere. Only the children were indifferent, and they adapted to this new life in spite of themselves—a life so different from the one we had spent in our home country.

There was nothing to do; we had to try to adapt. And we could not expect too much from those who had welcomed us. Canvas tents had been improvised and were used as sleeping rooms or shelters. We slept on the bare ground and in total darkness because the rooms did not contain field lamps.

In the mornings, it was difficult to bear the coolness of the Oubangui River, which was situated a few metres from the camp. We would wash there in the river at noon or in the afternoons. We also had to accept the food that UNHCR served us, defrosted and inedible dishes, fundamentally coarse. This made us sick, and some people, especially children, suffered from it with attacks of acute diarrhoea.

We also drank dirty water, which was not properly treated. As a result, we were not protected from other health hazards. Our health was being placed at risk, but what could we do about it? Nothing at all. We had to accept these brutal changes in life.

Sometime later, we were transferred to Mole, where the new shelter camp was set up. When we arrived there, things did not change at all. The same diet was maintained. After one month of settlement in Mole, more than five children had died because of this inhuman and degrading treatment.

When I left Bangui, I had more than 300,000 CFA francs. Part of this sum came from the money I had saved when I was working as a reporter for the *Agora* newspaper. Another part came from my property that I had sold, because I had gone back home to get it. Also, the friend I had travelled with had made up the rest. This money was spent in the camp to help us vary our diet.

By the beginning of September, we were beginning to get fed up with such a narrow and repetitive lifestyle. In the meantime, we had been mobilized to bury with dignity the dead children on the site. There was a health centre in the camp, but there were insufficient health workers—and those that were there were, above all else, incompetent. The only drug prescribed for children was Paracetamol, which could cure none of the ailments from which the children died.

Often, at night, it was difficult for us to sleep. And, as you know, Africa has its metaphysical, mystical realities that you cannot ignore. The site at Mole was really haunted. Evil spirits agitated the camp every night to the point where our nights were transformed into prayer vigils. Often, around midnight, the children started crying without stopping, and we knew straightaway that these spirits were already there. From everywhere, we heard cries of tears, murmurings of 'In the name of Jesus', to drive out these evil spirits.

As a result, our canvas tents were struck by invisible hands or feet, the echoes of which were actually felt. But why all this? According to reports, the inhabitants of Mole were hostile to our settlement there. And they were renowned in the practices of sorcery. In addition, some Central African refugees were beginning to flirt with Congolese girls, who were often married to their fellow Congolese citizens. This outraged the inhabitants of Mole, who considered us as 'invaders'. Our dear Central Africans were walking around with their asses in their heads, and the crisis had not prevented them from going into heat. They lusted after and ran around with Congolese girls, sometimes leading to the divorce of some couples. From these relationships were born illegitimate children, victims of the vices of our society.

Our activities consisted of eating, sleeping, and holding banal discussions—not to mention sex, which some refugees were so fond of as a way of passing the time. So our time was occupied with these banal things in order to escape our suffering. In addition, there were the striking stories of our experiences.

The story of a woman whose husband's and children's throats were slit was the most horrific. She wore a blood-stained dress that she refused to change despite the intervention of other women who were aware of her situation. She hardly spoke, and she was constantly crying. She had lost everything that was dearest to her, and her pain was difficult to bear.

The 300,000 CFA francs we had with us were starting to run out. However, we wanted to go to Kinshasa, as our life in the camp did not suit us. We had nurtured plans for the future, such as following our higher education; and the Congolese city that would allow us to realize this dream was Kinshasa— concerning which Congolese friends spoke very highly. They made us believe that there was a lot of opportunity in Kinshasa and that UNHCR was taking good care of urban refugees, offering at the same time education scholarships.

For us, going to Kinshasa was an opportunity for success. Thus, we decided to leave and get away from this wretched camp. To do so, on 22 September 2013, we took a public transit vehicle to begin our journey.

The route was Zongo–Gemena–Akula–Kinshasa. We arrived at Akula, where there is a large river port. From there, we took the boat to Kinshasa, a trip that lasted seven days.

Along our journey, we had serious problems with the immigration police. They turned us back several times on the grounds of irregularity in the administrative procedures which were to permit us to receive accommodation papers authorizing our travel to Kinshasa. In the middle of this hassle, we met a Congolese who had spent eight years in the Central African Republic. He was a seller at KM5. And as he heard us speak Sango (our national language) on the trip, he quickly established a connection with us to keep us company. He had already returned to his family in Kinshasa during the Boté coup in 2003.

Our new friend, Élie, decided to welcome us into his home in Kinshasa, where we would spend all the time of our exile. The immigration people had completely stripped us of the money we had on us, so from then on we could rely only on divine providence. A family of traders was travelling to Kinshasa on the same boat as we were. They fed us like little princes during the trip, as this family knew we were refugees. We feasted on fresh fish from the river, with roast meat and eggs prepared for the occasion. Every morning we had a large bowl of milk with delicious cakes.

Our trip on the boat was a success thanks to this family of traders, who showed us their generosity in the face of the ups and downs that we had overcome.

We finally arrived in Kinshasa, and Élie welcomed us into his home. However, he let us know straightaway that Kinshasa 'is another reality and that no one here takes care of anyone else'. It is 'every man for himself, and God for all'. It was here that our hell began.

After a day of rest, our friend Élie suggested that we go immediately to the factories in the square to find work, so as avoid starving in hardship. This we did. We negotiated fiercely, at the cost of multiple torments, so that we could be accepted in a plastics factory called OK Plast. We worked there like day labourers for six days in a row, for an income of 3,000 Congolese francs a day.

But it was difficult for us to get the team leaders to hire us regularly, since the local Congolese also had serious unemployment problems. The team leaders could not favour us— we were foreigners compared with the natives. Some 'positive discrimination' had to be put in place, so we had to bribe the team leaders to retain us.

UNHCR in Kinshasa refused to take care of us, saying that assistance to refugees was provided only at the refugee camp. Our situation became terrible, since no one supported us. As a result, we went through hard times.

I occasionally received money from my older sister who lives in Italy, but that could not cover everything as the cost of living was very high. We had gone up and down the majority of the factories in the Limeté Industriel, but only two factories had accepted us: OK Plast and OK Food.

Although I had my diplomas in law on me, it was difficult to get a job. So I went to ask at a Catholic radio station if I could be taken on as a freelance journalist. I was accepted after an interview with the programme director, who employed me as an editor in the newspaper section in French. I was given a fixed salary: 50 USD, which could not cover my needs; but I had no choice.

A lady had a restaurant in the radio station. Given my situation, she was obliged to give me free food every day. This really helped me. Her gesture is unforgettable. I will be forever grateful to her. I had to eat at this restaurant to also get some food for Olden, with whom I was living.

In addition, we went to several Protestant revival churches and others to explain our situation. People could not but sympathize with our plight, assisting us in various ways. We encountered the Compassion Church of Pastor Marcelo, where there was 'Le Restaurant du Cœur' for street children and the poor. We mixed in with them and went regularly to this restaurant to eat.

The church faithful also helped us financially. At times, they invited us to their homes to share family meals, during which we told them about the crisis in our country.

Other people in Kinshasa called us cannibals, monsters, and all kinds of bird names—because of what was relayed on the airwaves and social networks about the Central African Republic. They even refused to talk to us. They said we were 'inhuman', devils.

As things were not going well in Kinshasa and the security situation in Bangui started to improve, I decided to return home. I could not continue to live like this. So, I went to meet the UNHCR staff in Kinshasa so that I could be taken back to Mole camp, which would allow me to return easily to my country.

After going through the paperwork, I was scheduled for a free flight aboard a United Nations airplane. This flight was to Libenge; and from there, a UNHCR vehicle picked me up and brought me back to Mole camp. That same day, I took a motorcycle to go to Zongo. The same evening, around 6 p.m., I crossed by pirogue to Bangui.

Chapter 19

I returned home that evening, during a period when my country was slowly recovering from its crisis. I went to find some people I had left behind: my relatives, my friends, my acquaintances. Others were dead. People's gazes bore witness to the weight of the sufferings, sorrows, and pains endured during the crisis. And many of our material goods and other property had been destroyed.

I had to accept the country's situation and try to start from scratch; therefore, I had to find an activity to occupy my time. I returned to work as a reporter for the *Agora* newspaper. From there, I participated actively in the preparations for the presidential and legislative elections, which successfully led to the return to constitutional order. Thus, I created my blog to try to reach the general public and to increase the visibility of my journalism activities.

However, my monthly earnings did not allow me to live on my business, as I earned only between 18 and 20 USD a week. As a result, I was tempted to find something better elsewhere. Then I found work at IRAD, a national NGO which is a subcontractor to OXFAM. I was retained there as a coordinator of hygiene. My main task was to coordinate the sewage disposal activities at the various sites of displaced persons in Bangui, where latrines had been built to allow the displaced to satisfy their needs—in order to prevent the spread of epidemics, such as cholera. We took regular care of the latrines so that they were not filled up and stinking the place out. In addition to that, we did private disposal of waste to meet the needs of individuals, as we were the only organization working in this area. I resigned after a few months of this work.

I learned from displaced people when they began to speak about the tragedies they had undergone and the difficulties they could have in moving on with their lives. Some had lost almost everything, having nothing left to connect them with this life—especially those that came from Boying, Miskine, and even KM5. Women were obviously the most vulnerable, as they were forced to feed themselves through working on the streets as prostitutes. I was really disturbed by the account of a woman who, to feed her family, could prostitute herself with five to ten men a day for a sum of 100 CFA francs per interaction. This was how sexually transmitted diseases spread easily.

All these evils have their origins in the bad organization of our society, where politics does not favour the equality of all before the public services of the state, or the integration of all communities in the process of national development. There are Muslim and Christian parents on all sides, and the real religious war begins in our respective homes. People hide behind these community identities to push our people to engage in large-scale genocide. It is a pity that this works so well in the Central African Republic.

Interlude III: What's the point?

What's the point of screaming if your voice isn't
heard?
What's the point of fighting if your struggle
Is like a drop of water in the sea?
What's the point of denouncing these appalling
crimes if those
Who support them are right at our bedside?
What's the point of having the black community
at our head
If it is indifferent and contributes to the decline
of our country?
What's the point of retaining MINUSCA if our
crisis
Has to feed it and rob us?
What's the point of having a president if he or
she
Is an arse-licker?
What's the point of hoping if there are still
Weapons under our beds?
What's the point of staying if our situation
Deteriorates more and more?
What's the point of getting started
If darkness obscures the end of the tunnel?
What's the point of living if our daily lives
Are kneaded with misfortune and tears?
What's the point of thinking if
The next day we will have the same fate?
What's the point of sleeping if

Don't you know whether you'll ever wake up
again?
What's the point of loving if
Death will soon separate us?
We're just asking ourselves one question:
Are we aware of the disintegration
Of our nation?

Lucius said: 'No wind is favourable for those who do not know where they are going.' For many years now, the Central African people have been in agony, bearing the pain of the crisis. And no one knows at this time where this crisis is leading us, since neither the government nor MINUSCA seems to be up to the task of remedying the situation.

We cannot have two captains on a ship

J. Rousseau said: 'I would wish then that no one in the state could say of himself that he was above the law, and that no one could impose on the state an obligation to recognize this; for, whatever may be the constitution of a government, if it is not subject to the law, all others are necessarily at the discretion of that government; and if there is a national leader and another, foreign leader—whatever share of authority they may take—it is impossible for one and the other to be properly obeyed and for the state to be well governed.'

Rousseau's thinking clearly fits the crisis our country is going through, where two different entities are proposing to resolve it: MINUSCA on the one hand, and the Central African government on the other. And we have seen both of them at work, groping in vain for how to resolve it. The simple reason is that there are two captains on our ship. As a result, the government cannot be properly controlled. One of them must give up his authority in favour of a single centre of decision-making, whose vision and management will be focussed on a rigorous resolution of the crisis.

MINUSCA has available the means of war to maintain and impose peace in the Central African Republic. But there is no political will on its part for the full implementation of its mandate, such that killings and massacres continue to paralyse the country.

Also, when Rousseau says, 'If there is a national leader and another, foreign leader—whatever share of authority they may take—it is impossible for one and the other to be properly obeyed and for the state to be well governed'—this demonstrates in our case that some rebel groups act at the discretion of MINUSCA, as they can kill and massacre with the full knowledge of and under the noses of UN forces. To justify impunity, MINUSCA advocates the need for a peaceful resolution of the crisis. It is intolerable that people are killed under the noses of UN troops. So, what is the reason for their presence in the country? This demonstrates complicity, sabotage, indifference. The security of the people is the main responsibility of the government and not of MINUSCA.

Many Central Africans thought that the visit of the UN Secretary General would change the course of events. But despite this visit, punctuated by interviews with politicians, rebels, and clerics, the acts of violence do not stop getting worse in the provinces.

A Balaka resident said: 'The war between the UPC and the FPRC is a war of vested interests. They fight to rape and loot and to take over mining sites and strategic positions .... All the other reasons provided are nothing more than pretexts.' And MINUSCA is better placed to understand this reality; but it prefers to accommodate the subversive actions of armed groups that hide behind Christian or Muslim identities to maintain the crisis. Also, the country's natural resources illegally exploited by these groups are known to MINUSCA, which butters them up.

MINUSCA always acts like a mocking fireman, once people kill each other in abundance. What is the reason for the mission of this cursed system, where sacrificed human lives have to be used as a reason to maintain it, while it itself is absolutely useless.

In MINUSCA's report regarding human rights violations and abuses and the violation of international humanitarian law by rebel groups, it specified the bases of these armed groups as well as their malignant force. MINUSCA therefore knows the perpetrators of the crimes it encounters on a daily basis in the course of its patrols, but nevertheless it fails to gain the upper hand over them. It is clear that the UN Security Council's resolutions and Chapter VII of its treaty are simply trampled underfoot.

MINUSCA's intentional inability encourages armed groups to perpetrate acts of violence and massacres—as they can kill, rape, steal, loot, set fire to entire villages, and return to Bangui to celebrate their billions, escorted by MINUSCA.

And yes, the principle is simple: no crisis, no UN mission. We must therefore maintain the crisis to keep this cursed system alive. Because we eat there, we screw there, we kill there, we rape there. That's life and it's too bad for the victims. They will find themselves in hell 'another day', but above all they must live on Central African blood. It is delicious blood. They have everything to gain: gold, diamonds, and women and children to rape. Long live MINUSCA!

The process of disarmament, demobilization, reintegration, and repatriation must be launched immediately, so that the state owes nothing to anyone—in order to be free to govern. Apart from this ideal, no other claim, nothing illegal, can be taken into account as a grounds for destabilization.

1. Lifting the embargo: The redeployment of the FACA

If the embargo[12] was the solution to the problems of Central Africa, the crisis would never continue. It is clear that the government is demeaning only itself by bowing before the embargo—while rebel groups are acquiring thousands of weapons, from sources well known to the international community. This

[12] A UN arms embargo imposed in 2013 was partially lifted for Moscow at the end of 2017, yet renewed in early 2018 for one year.

embargo would be beneficial to us *if* all the parties respected it.

The government is powerless in the face of armed incursions and violence because of its inaction. This injustice maintained by the international community for the benefit of the rebels proves in itself that the embargo has no justification, other than that it contributes to the aggravation of the suffering of the Central African people. Therefore, the embargo must be lifted so that the government's responsibility for matters of security can be fully implemented.

To do this, the government must create 'buffer zones' or 'no-go areas' at the borders and in areas at risk. The borders must be controlled once and for all, and territorial integrity must be defended. And in troubled areas or cities, the security forces must be deployed to protect the people and repel armed attacks. No rebel group has the right to massacre the population with impunity, to the indifference of the government and of MINUSCA. Moreover, I would like to stop consulting MINUSCA, whose security staff clearly state: 'We haven't left our families, our loved ones to die in the Central African Republic.' Therefore, they are here just to enrich themselves, to drive luxury cars, and not to assist in the restoration of the Central African Republic. We must take responsibility for our own safety and, if possible, save our skins. This is the price of our deliverance.

Moreover, our armed forces must behave responsibly, with dignity and neutrality in resolving the crisis. Neither bias nor revenge must follow from their actions in order to achieve unity and social cohesion once and for all.

2. The social component

The social component is the most important of all. A new vision must be drawn up for the Central African Republic, a vision marked by concrete actions and not by empty words and hollow speeches—because those who have suffered most from the crisis are the poor. They have also been led into acts of violence and massacres to escape the reality of their lives.

The social component must be more prominent at the end of the crisis, for it is from the hearts of men that vain projects are fomented. These projects are the result of social inequalities, injustices, and marginalization. This is what the state must tackle, to heal the wounds of broken hearts, to reconcile people to one another—in order to give them a sense of responsibility and integrate them effectively.

The crisis has destroyed almost everything in the country; there is absolutely nothing left in the form of basic social structures in the provinces, such that the daily lives of the people have become a living hell. There are no schools, no hospitals, no public administrations. Thus, the state must be able to restore meaning to people's lives by continuing or supporting emergency humanitarian activities to provide relief. It is certainly true that we should move beyond humanitarian needs to make a start on national recovery and development, but this humanitarian emergency process cannot be undermined at once—because of the great challenges and expectations of the people. We need to strengthen the resilience capacities of these grassroots communities where the crisis is most experienced.

3. The economic component

The Central African Republic is 'the land of the riches of the heart'. It is not possible for its people to live below their privileges, in unparalleled poverty. We are prized for our riches; and we are massacred at the same time for the same riches—and now we cannot fully enjoy them.

Good governance, transparency, and the equal distribution of the country's riches must determine from now on the government's actions. The country is currently receiving significant assistance. But it must be used well so that it can have a significant impact on people's lives. There is no longer a question of tolerating the misappropriation of public funds and money laundering, both of which damage the recovery of the economy.

Therefore, the state must create wealth and employment, economic opportunities for the unemployed—especially for young people—in order to prevent them from returning to arms. To do this, the state must think about major economic reforms to attract foreign investment. In addition, it must build, rehabilitate, and develop economic infrastructure, and it must recapture and control mining areas to boost its public and customs revenues—in particular revenues on diamond, gold, and timber exports.

4. The political component

The current government must unite all the people around the ideals of reconstruction, social cohesion, unity, and peace. It must therefore think about opening up to other significant political sensitivities, to navigate everyone in this ship of national harmony. Also, the political parties and the various opponents must avoid pointless dissension, in order to contribute to the return of a definitive peace.

5. The justice component

I am not a supporter of impunity. So I do not really appreciate amnesty as a means of resolving a crisis. This has created habits whose marks we now bear. All criminals and warlords must be placed in prison, to be held accountable for their actions. The judicial system must therefore be put in place to investigate, interrogate, and prosecute all perpetrators of crimes from 2003 to the present day.

Printed in the United States
By Bookmasters